ANIMAL
ALERT

KILLER ON THE LOOSE

Animal Alert series

1 Intensive Care
2 Abandoned
3 Killer on the Loose
4 Quarantine
5 Skin and Bone
6 Crash
7 Blind Alley
8 Living Proof
9 Grievous Bodily Harm
10 Running Wild

ANIMAL
ALERT

KILLER ON THE LOOSE

Jenny Oldfield

Hodder
Children's
Books

a division of Hodder Headline plc

Special thanks to David Brown and Margaret Marks of Leeds
RSPCA Animal Home and Clinic, and to Raj Duggal M.V.Sc.,
M.R.C.V.S. and Louise Kinvig B.V.M.S., M.R.C.V.S.

Visit Jenny Oldfield's website at
www.testware.co.uk/jenny oldfield

Text copyright © 1997 Jenny Oldfield
Illustrations copyright © 1997 Trevor Parkin

First published in Great Britain in 1997
by Hodder Children's Books

British Library Cataloguing in Publication Data
A record for this book is available from the British Library

ISBN 0 340 68171 3

Typeset by Avon Dataset Ltd, Bidford-on-Avon, Warks

Printed and bound in Great Britain by
The Guernsey Press Co. Ltd, Guernsey, Channel Islands

Hodder and Stoughton
a division of Hodder Headline plc
338 Euston Road
London NW1 3BH

Foreword

Tess, my eight-year-old border collie, has been injured by a speeding car. I rush her to the vet's. The doors of the operating theatre swing open, a glimpse of bright lights and gleaming instruments, then, 'Don't worry, we'll do everything we can for her,' a kind nurse promises, shepherding me away . . .

Road traffic accidents, stray dogs, sad cases of cruelty and neglect: spend a day in any busy city surgery and watch the vets and nurses make their vital, split-second decisions. If, like me, you've ever owned or longed to own an animal, you'll admire as much as I do the work of these dedicated people. And you'll know from experience exactly what the owners in my *Animal Alert* stories are going through. Luckily for me, Tess came safely through her operation, but endings aren't always so happy . . .

Jenny Oldfield
19 March 1997

1

Paul Grey worked fast to deliver the kittens. 'Give me a hand, Carly,' he said as he made an incision into the unconscious animal's abdomen. He put down the shiny scalpel and Carly handed him a suction tube to clear the blood which spurted from the wound.

Bright lights shone on to the operating table, the mother cat was out cold. She was a fine pedigree, a Russian Blue, and the birth had always promised to be difficult. Carly's dad had decided on a Caesarean section at fifty-eight days, when he saw that the cat's blood pressure was too high for a normal delivery.

'OK, now when I lift the first one out, I need you standing by with a towel,' he told Carly. 'I'll break the sac and you rub the kitten down. That way we'll encourage it to start breathing.'

Carly concentrated hard. There was nothing pretty about a newborn kitten fresh from the birth sac. It was slimy, blind and helpless. But as her dad drew the first one out of the womb and handed it to her, she began to rub. 'Come on!' she urged, holding her own breath until she saw the first intake of air. The tiny body shuddered into life.

'Well done.' Paul Grey was already lifting out the second kitten. 'Now nip the umbilical cord between your thumb and forefinger.'

She wasn't squeamish, so went ahead and did as she was told. She knew that tearing the cord was better than snipping it because the kitten lost less blood. She put the tiny, blind creature into a plastic box lined with newspapers and a warm blanket. Then it was time to move on to deal with the second kitten as her father passed it to her.

They delivered five kittens in this way; each one alive and healthy, though Paul Grey said they were, as he'd expected, a bit on the small side.

'Cleopatra's only a young cat herself, and I could see she wouldn't be able to carry the kittens to full term,' he told Carly quietly as he finished delivering them and began to sew up the incisions. 'Luckily we've done the section in good time. All five should be fine!'

Carly sighed with relief. The string on her surgical mask pulled the dark hair at the nape of her neck, her forehead was moist with sweat. The lights glared down on the unconscious patient.

'Are they all safely in the incubator?'

She nodded. 'Can I do anything else to help?'

'No. I'm finishing off here. Cleopatra will start coming round soon. You take a breather. Come back with a glucose and water mixture for her to drink in ten minutes.' He lifted the mother cat from the operating table and put her carefully inside a separate plastic cage.

'Shall I hose down the table?' Still she hovered, checking that the five kittens were alive. They squirmed on the blanket, eyes closed, looking like little drowned rats.

'No. I'll get Mel to do it before she leaves.' He looked up. 'Scram, Carly. Go on!'

Reluctantly she untied her mask and took off her green plastic surgical gown. She threw them in the bin by the door. 'Can I give the owner the news?'

'Sure. Tell her that Cleopatra's the proud mother of five perfect kittens: two males and three females.'

'Thanks to you.' Carly grinned at him. He was bending over the cat, checking her pulse, waiting for her to come round.

'All part of the job,' he insisted.

'One of the best parts!' Helping at a birth, being there when new life came into the world. Carly loved it. She dashed through to reception to deliver the good news.

'Mrs Simms?' Bupinda called the name of Cleopatra's owner from her position behind the reception desk. She held the telephone in one hand, shifted papers with the other, calm as ever.

A woman jumped up from the bench by the window, her long wait over. 'I'm Bonnie Simms!'

Carly went to meet her. 'Cleopatra's had her kittens. Five of them. They're all fine.'

'Oh, thank heavens! And what about Cleo?'

'She's fine too. The operation went without a hitch.'

'Can I see them?' Bonnie Simms drew a deep breath; a woman in her thirties, with short dark hair, hazel eyes and a full mouth which spread now into a wide smile.

Carly nodded. 'Pretty soon, I expect. Dad has to wait for Cleo to come round, then he'll be out to let us know.' She felt proud as the eyes of other pet owners in the waiting area focused on them.

'I was so worried about her,' Bonnie Simms went on in a rush of relief. 'This is her first litter. She's only just over a year old. I gave her loads of extra vitamins and minerals, but Mr Grey said that could have been a mistake, especially the calcium. Extra calcium makes for big-boned kittens, which of course is a problem for a small cat . . .'

She ran out of breath and allowed Carly to

jump in at last. 'The kittens are a bit small actually.' Mrs Simms was obviously a caring owner who knew plenty about looking after cats.

'That's the problem with breeding pedigrees; you often get complications that you wouldn't normally find in your common-or-garden moggy!'

'Do you breed Russian Blues?' Carly loved Cleo's unusual colour. These cats were long and handsome, pure grey with bright green eyes.

'I've just started. Cleo is my first queen, but I've had the tomcat, Rameses, for two years now.' Bonnie Simms was keen to tell Carly all about her cats. 'We live up the road in a house over-looking the park. I don't let them out at the front of the house in case they wander on to the main road, but they can go out the back way – except when Cleo is on heat, of course. Then I keep her in, and every tomcat in the neighbourhoood comes calling!' She chatted on, glancing anxiously at the doors behind the desk, where Paul Grey was reviving Cleo.

'Not long now,' Carly promised.

And here came her dad, tugging off his mask,

pushing through the doors, coming to con-
gratulate Bonnie Simms, who was pleased and
relieved all over again, as she went through with
the vet to take her first look at the kittens, leaving
Carly in reception to help Bupinda deal with the
last few patients of the evening.

They sent a black Labrador called Susie into
treatment room number two to have her nails
clipped by assistant vet, Liz Hutchins. Susie's feet
rattled noisily on the shiny floor tiles as she
waddled in for treatment. Then there was a tabby
kitten for routine jabs and an old spaniel with a
heart murmur. Carly went in and out, from
reception to treatment room, standing in for their
nurse, Mel, who had just left work to keep a
dentist's appointment.

'Nearly through,' Liz told her, after she'd filled
out a prescription for the spaniel. Though she
was a qualified vet, she was fresh out of college,
and she treated Carly as an equal. With her
sandy-coloured hair, slight Scottish accent and
her lively style, she was a breath of fresh air at
Beech Hill.

'Don't speak too soon,' Bupinda warned. From

her desk she had a good view of the main entrance.

Carly popped her head out of the treatment room. 'Wasn't that our final patient?' She was hoping to nip upstairs to the flat to feed Ruby, Beech Hill's own 'common-or-garden' moggy.

'Yes, but here comes a last-minute case.'

'Tell them to come back tomorrow. We're closed!' Liz called. Dusk was falling after a long and tiring day.

'Oh, hang on a minute, I was wrong. It's not a patient, it's Hoody.'

At the sound of his name, Carly shot out to check. 'Has he brought Vinny with him?'

'Yep.'

Vinny was her friend's mongrel dog. Rough, tough Vinny – part bull-terrier, part something else – was one of Carly's favourite animals. She ran to the door to meet him.

There he was, with his short brindle coat, his white chest and bandy-legged walk, trotting across the carpark. Hoody followed quickly, carrying a bundle in his arms.

Carly looked again – was it just an old jacket?

8

No. From the look on Hoody's face, she realised this was serious. She opened the door and ran out.

'Look what I found!' he gasped. He unwrapped the edge of the jacket and let her see what he was carrying.

What she saw made Carly wince. There was a dog inside the jacket, but she couldn't see what sort because of the blood which covered its whole face. The dark muzzle was torn and gashed, the jaw seemed to have slid to one side and be hanging loose. 'Quick!' She urged Hoody and Vinny inside. 'What happened?'

'Dunno. I just found him in the park.'

'Is he still alive?' Carly called for Liz.

'He'd better be!' Hoody handed the whole bundle over to Carly. He stood there in jeans and T-shirt, breathing hard after his race to the Rescue Centre. 'That's another jacket ruined,' he grumbled. This wasn't the first injured dog he'd bought in from the park.

'Wait here.' She moved fast, carrying the dog into a treatment room. 'Tell us about it after!'

'Yeah, yeah. Like, I've got all day,' he muttered.

But Carly knew he would hang around anyway.

'What is it, an RTA?' Liz followed Carly into the room as she laid the dog on a table.

'Don't think so. Hoody found him in the park.'

Carefully Liz removed the bloody jacket and dropped it in a bin. The dog lay shivering and panting, his eyes half closed. Soon a fresh trickle of blood dribbled from his injured mouth. 'No cars in the park, eh?' She examined the jaw and the deep cuts on his face. 'If it's not a traffic accident, it could be another so-called mystery attack, I suppose.'

Too concerned to ask Liz for details, Carly watched her run expert fingers over the dog's ribs, abdomen and pelvis. Now that he was free of the jacket, she could make out that this was a small Jack Russell terrier; mostly white-haired, with patches of black and brown. His stumpy body quivered from nose to tail. He made no noise as Liz examined him.

'Bad shock,' Liz said quietly. 'And he's lost a lot of blood.' She concentrated on the jaw once more. 'Fractured. Someone's used a lot of force to do this.'

Carly gritted her teeth. 'Any other broken bones?'

'Not so far as I can tell. We'll stop the bleeding, give him a pain-killer, then put him on a drip and keep him quiet overnight. Then we'll X-ray him tomorrow morning.' Gently she turned the dog on to his other side. 'You see this rapid breathing?'

Carly noticed the shallow panting, the pink tongue sliding sideways out of the mouth.

'That's trauma. His heart's racing. Let's hope the shock hasn't weakened it.' She looked around for a collar to check for a name and telephone number. 'That's odd,' she commented when she couldn't find one.

'I'll go and ask Hoody.' Carly slipped out of the room. She felt her own heart beating fast at what she'd just seen.

In reception, Hoody's scowling face greeted her. Vinny sat quietly at his side. 'He's not dead, is he?'

She shook her head. 'Not quite.' It was typical of him to think the worst. 'Don't blame us. We're the ones who are trying to help, remember.'

'Sorry.' He shrugged.

'There's no collar, so we don't know who he is or where he came from.'

'Here.' Sliding his hand into his pocket, Hoody drew out a thin leather strap. 'I took it off in case it stopped him from breathing properly.'

Carly took the collar and read the words on the small brass disc.

'His name's Russ, he lives on King Edward's Road, and there's a telephone number as well,' Hoody told her in his offhand way.

Now the dog had a name and an owner. Someone somewhere must be frantic with worry. She handed the collar to Bupinda, who picked up the phone to ring the number.

'I asked you, was he dead, and you said not quite,' Hoody reminded Carly. 'What do you mean exactly?'

'Broken jaw, severe shock, lost a lot of blood.' Absent-mindedly patting Vinny's head, she ran through the problems. 'His face has been practically torn apart!'

'Ouch!' He grimaced.

'Yep,' she agreed. 'It's pretty bad. So where did

you find him?' She was glad that Hoody had played the hero and brought in an injured dog. He might act tough, as if he couldn't care less, but Carly knew this was only for show.

'Like I said, in the park.'

'Yes, but whereabouts in the park?' It was a big area, an open space in the middle of the inner city, with soccer pitches, gardens, a long, narrow lake.

'Across the other side, near those council stores.'

'But not near the road?' Getting information from Hoody was always hard. You had to squeeze out every drop.

'What is this? Did I miss something? Have I been arrested?'

'No, I didn't mean it to sound that way. Only, I'm upset.' She was half afraid for poor Russ's chances, half mad at the person who had done this to him.

'You're not the only one.'

'What do you mean?'

'There were loads of people out there, a whole crowd. All staring at him lying there and saying

13

wasn't it terrible and hadn't somebody better fetch a vet?'

'But you were the only one who did anything?' Carly noticed Bupinda put down the phone with an exasperated sigh. She hadn't been able to get through to Russ's owner.

'Someone had to.' Hoody went to stare out of the window overlooking the carpark. Obedient Vinny followed him. 'You should have heard them carrying on about it.'

'What do you mean? What were they saying . . . ? Sorry!' She backed off from asking more questions.

'Get this,' he said, still staring out of the window. 'The word is, there's a killer on the loose out there.'

'A *what*?'

'A killer. Some sort of wild animal. You know what people are like.'

'But what are they on about?' Carly couldn't figure it out. Was this what Liz had meant by a 'mystery attack'?

'OK, this is the story.' Hoody turned. He made it clear he didn't believe a word of it himself.

'This killer is supposed to be a wolf!'

'That's stupid!' Carly snorted. 'We don't have wolves in the wild in Britain!'

'I know that. But that's what they're saying. This animal, whatever it is, has been seen by quite a few people. They swear that's what it is!'

'Who's "they"?' Carly felt like jumping to the defence of the unknown creature, whatever it was. Sometimes people could make really stupid mistakes.

'The ones who've seen it,' Hoody said, annoyingly calm. 'Look, you'd better ask them yourself.' He was getting ready to leave, realising that he'd done all he could for now.

'But it's just gossip. Don't they know that?' Anyway, who exactly was she supposed to ask? With wild rumours flying around, getting to the bottom of what had happened to Russ was going to be hard.

'Says you,' Hoody reminded her.

'You don't believe them, do you?'

For a while Hoody paused, his hand on the door, ready to push out into the cool evening air.

'Nope,' he decided, shoving through the door at last. Vinny trotted on ahead. 'But if it wasn't a wolf, you tell me what on earth *did* rip that poor dog's face to shreds!'

2

'Any word from Russ's owner yet?' Carly's dad popped his tousled head into Reception as he came downstairs from the flat. It was eight the following morning; a Thursday in late August.

'I'm still trying!' Bupinda had just dialled the number again. 'No answer so far.'

'Carly, how about helping me feed the new kittens?' This was Mel, calling down from the first-floor small-animal unit. 'You know, the Russian Blues!'

'Brilliant!' She dropped the tidying job she was doing for Bupinda.

'Hey, what about these case notes?' The receptionist swung her long black plait behind her shoulder and lodged the phone under her chin.

'Later!' Carly promised. She shot upstairs to help Mel instead.

Cleo's five kittens lay snuggled in their box under an infrared lamp. Carly checked the temperature inside the box to see that it kept to a steady ninety degrees. Their eyes were still closed, but they nuzzled and snuffled inside the blanket, giving high, hungry cries.

'Hold your horses!' Mel cried, as she prepared the formula kitten feed. 'We're coming, we're coming!'

Carly scrubbed her hands at the sink and checked the whiteboard to see that the kittens had last been fed three hours earlier, at five. 'Who did it at that time?' she wanted to know.

'Your dad, I expect.' Mel hummed a tune from the charts as she worked. 'He probably got up twice during the night. How did he look this morning?'

'Terrible.' His wavy brown hair had been sticking out all over the place, he had bags under his eyes and his breakfast had consisted of nothing but black coffee.

Mel tutted. 'Who'd be a vet?'

'Me!' It was Carly's big ambition. 'How's poor Cleo?'

'Fine. Enjoying the rest, no doubt. She might as well make the most of it. She'll be feeding the kittens herself by the end of the day!' The nurse took out the first kitten and slid a plastic dropper into his mouth. She waited for him to begin to suck. 'There's another dropper on the tray, whenever you're ready,' she told Carly briskly.

So she joined in the kitten-feeding session, enjoying the squirm of the hot little bodies as they nestled one by one in her lap and took the milk. Each would feed, then she would gently massage the abdomen, imitating the licking of the mother cat so that the kitten's digestive system would work properly. After that, the kitten would be put back into the box where the litter would stay warm and safe until Cleo had recovered from her op.

The delicate job took about half an hour, and Mel seized the opportunity to sit and chat. 'I hear we've got a Jack Russell in a bad state downstairs. I haven't had chance to see him yet, but I heard about it in the pub last night, of all places. You should have heard the gossip. Apparently there's a dangerous animal on the loose. It sounds horrendous! You'd better keep a special eye on Ruby for a bit!'

Carly said nothing. These rumours spread fast.

'Big, bad and ugly!' Mel went on. 'Like something out of a horror movie. The Beast of Beech Hill! Everyone was talking about it.'

'Hoody brought him in. He was the only one there with any sense.' Carly stuck to the facts. 'Bupinda's still trying to contact the owner.'

'Will Paul be able to operate?'

'He doesn't know yet. He'll have to X-ray the dog's jaw first. But we're waiting until we've got in touch with the owner and told him or her what we have to do.' Talk of Russ made her anxious. As soon as they'd finished with the kittens, she ran back down to reception, where patients were trickling in for morning surgery.

'Well?' she demanded.

Bupinda nodded. 'It's a Mr Price. He gave us the go-ahead and he's on his way here. Your dad and Liz are in the operating theatre now.'

Carly swung through the double doors into the sterile room whose walls were lined with instrument trolleys, anaesthetic machines and resuscitation equipment. The two vets were already hard at work.

Liz looked up as she came in. 'X-ray showed a compound fracture of the jaw,' she told Carly. 'We'll need to wire it back together.'

Carly grimaced. It would mean drilling through the bone, rebuilding the jaw so that the dog would be able to use it properly once it was healed. 'What are his chances?' she asked, putting on her mask and standing by, ready to help.

'Pretty good,' her dad said. He never got up-tight over his work, always worked smoothly and calmly.

Sometimes Carly thought he didn't have a single nerve in his body. She felt herself wince now as she looked closely at the poor dog's shattered jaw.

'You OK?' Liz asked.

She nodded. Usually she coped well with the daily routine of injuries and sickness, but this was really bad. Carly's head felt dizzy and she drew a deep breath.

'You're not as thick-skinned as you like to think,' Liz reminded her. 'Look, we'll manage here. You go out and help Bupinda talk to Mr Price when he gets here.'

For once Carly let herself be edged out of the operating theatre, knowing that she wouldn't be much use if she stayed. Taking off her mask, she stepped outside, putting on a brave face when she saw Hoody hanging about with Vinny in reception.

'How is he?' he asked. No 'Hi!', no smile of greeting.

'He's stable. But his jawbone looks like a jigsaw. They're piecing it back together right now.' Her voice was fainter than she wanted it to be. By this time, the waiting room was full of people with their sick dogs and cats, their pregnant guinea-pigs and moulting budgerigars.

Steve stood at Bupinda's desk, talking to

the receptionist and nurse. They were flicking through some files.

'Steve's got this new theory,' Hoody explained.

Hearing his name mentioned, Steve beckoned them both across. 'Mel's been telling me about this rumour that's flying around,' he explained. 'About the so-called wolf.'

'You don't believe that, do you?' Carly and Hoody said together.

'I think it's unlikely,' he agreed. 'We'd know if a wolf had escaped in transit to a zoo or a safari park. Mind you, some people might be daft enough to keep one as a pet, like they keep lion cubs, as a kind of status symbol.' He leafed through a pile of folders, looking for the ones he wanted.

'That's cruel!' Carly protested. Wild animals belonged in the wild.

'And usually illegal,' Steve agreed. 'But when did *that* stop some people?' At last he held up a folder. 'This is it; a record of some other recent mystery attacks in the area. Look, three dogs have been brought in with unexplained injuries since the start of the summer. All of them were attacked on this side of town.' He showed the others the case notes.

'One at the end of June,' Bupinda read, 'two in July, and now Russ.'

'And there's a kind of pattern.' Carly picked up on the details. 'These dogs have all been brought in late in the evening, or very early in the morning, and there's never been an owner on the scene to tell us what's happened. Two of them were strays.' One had died from its wounds, the other two had recovered.

Steve looked thoughtfully through the notes. 'Similar injuries. Whatever is doing this goes for the face and throat. I'd say it was probably the work of the same style of attacker, if not the self-same one each time.'

Mel nodded and looked serious. 'Maybe the rumour's right,' she said quietly. 'The Beast of Beech Hill really *does* exist!'

'Shh!' Hoody warned her to keep her voice down. People waiting in the queue were begin-ning to get curious.

'What do you think?' Carly asked Steve.

'Well, there's a spate of unexplained incidents,

that's for sure,' he said cautiously. He was a softly spoken man who'd been an inspector for three years. Patience made him good at his job, and helped him stick with a case until he had unravelled all the clues. 'We've only got one other owner on record here.' Extracting a piece of paper from the file, he folded it and put it in his pocket. 'I think I'd better look her up later today; see what I can find out.'

'You want to make some links?' Hoody was interested in the way he worked. This appealed to him more than the wild rumours. 'Maybe you could find out if anyone's actually seen one of these attacks happening.'

'Exactly!' Carly agreed. Until then they shouldn't jump to conclusions.

'Actually, someone has!' Mel jumped in, eager as ever.

'What, seen an attack?' Hoody challenged.

'Yes. They were telling me in the pub last night. Not this latest one, but the one in June. It happened on the edge of an industrial estate by Fiveways, didn't it? You know, lots of grotty scrubland, piles of rubble. The dog was well-known round there; it was a scruffy little cross-breed of some sort. A few people fed it scraps. A girl I know works in an office there, and she said she went in early one morning and heard this terrible noise outside. She looked out of the window, but it was still a bit misty, so she couldn't see anything clearly. But she saw enough!' The nurse paused, her eyes wide, pushing her long red hair back from her forehead, waiting for their reaction.

'Come on then, tell us!' Hoody was impatient.

'She saw this shape in the mist. According to her, it was snarling and slavering, having a real go at the poor stray dog.'

'What did it look like?' Carly asked.

'Pointed ears, long nose, a big, thick neck, bushy tail.'

'How big?' It was Steve's turn to quiz Mel.

'Bigger than a dog. Like a German shepherd, but bigger, definitely.' She spoke as if she was quite certain. 'More like a wolf.'

Hoody groaned and turned away. He muttered under his breath.

'What's up? I'm only telling you what she said.

Big and vicious. She called a security man and he scared it off with a long metal pole. He swore it looked like a wolf too. Anyway, it left the poor stray in a terrible mess. She phoned me here at Beech Hill and that's when Steve stepped in.' She reminded them of the sequence of events.

'OK, let's keep an open mind if we can,' Steve insisted. 'I can go and have another word with your friend, find out more. What's her name?'

'Sharon Charlton.'

The inspector jotted down a few more details.

Meanwhile, Carly saw Hoody make for the exit with Vinny and followed him outside. 'What's eating you?' she demanded.

'Nothing. I'm busy, that's all.'

'In the summer holidays?'

'Yep, I've got better things to do than listen to that stuff.'

Mel's story and Russ's injuries had rattled her. She turned on Hoody. 'Well, you started it!'

'Me?' He glared back.

'Yes. If you hadn't come in here yesterday and told us all that stupid gossip in the park, no one would be thinking this way right now!' He was the one who'd mentioned a killer on the loose.

'So it's my fault?'

'You know what people are like!'

'So? What are you so mad about anyway?'

'I'm not mad!'

'Hah!' He laughed in her face, strode off across the carpark. Vinny trotted at his heels. 'Don't blame me because some dog's lying in there with its face torn apart. Blame Mel. She's the one with the big imagination!'

Carly watched him storm off. She wanted to cry, she wanted to yell and shout. *Why can't we just get on with looking after animals? Why do we have to get dragged into stories about wolves?* The whole thing had knocked her off balance and now she was blaming Hoody.

Stupid, stupid! she said to herself, to the world in general.

Bonnie Simms appeared at the gate and hurried towards Carly, a worried look on her face, a folded newspaper clutched in her hand.

Hoody stumbled into Cleo's owner in his hurry. Vinny yapped and skipped sideways out of the way. The boy swore and gave his parting shot. 'You're crazy, you know that?' he yelled at Carly. Then he turned the corner and was gone.

3

A reporter from the local paper had got on to the story. There it was, in big black letters across the front page: MYSTERY BEAST AT LARGE!

Bonnie Simms had brought it in to show them at the Rescue Centre as soon as it had landed on her doormat. 'Have you seen this?' she asked Paul Grey, who had just finished the surgery on Russ. 'I was coming in anyway to see Cleo and the kittens, and I knew you'd be interested.'

Carly glimpsed the newspaper article between the elbows and over the shoulders of the people who had crowded round the desk to look. 'Savage attack . . . unknown owner . . . heroic rescue by local boy!'

'Fancy it making the headline news!' a woman from the queue in the waiting room gasped.

'They're saying it's like the wild cat that was spotted on Bodmin Moor in Devon, the one that causes the farmers all that trouble!' someone else said. 'They never found out exactly what that was, did they?'

'A puma,' the first woman said. 'It was supposed to be interbreeding with the feral cats down there. Now there are dozens of them, apparently.'

'Does it say what ours looks like?' Mel craned her neck to see. She couldn't get near the desk to read.

Bonnie Simms nodded. 'There's a description. They say it's much too big to be a domestic breed of dog; well over seventy centimetres tall. They've got an eye-witness saying it was pale grey, with big jaws and long legs. Listen: "I saw it loping away from the scene of the attack," says 28-year-old Theresa Worthing of Beacon Street. "There was blood on its mouth. It must have reached a speed of over thirty kilometres an hour as it cut across the park, towards the lake. Then it vanished in some bushes." ' She read out part of the article, stabbing the paper with her fingertip.

'At least we can be sure ours isn't a puma,' Paul Grey said quietly. He winked at Carly. 'I suppose a wolf makes a change.'

'Anything else?' Bupinda asked.

Bonnie read on. 'The journalist asked an expert what it was likely to be, from the description the eye-witness had given. She said it sounded similar to a wild dog which had terrorised some farms on the Welsh borders. She didn't think it was likely to be an actual wolf.'

'At least *someone*'s talking sense.' Carly's dad tried to quieten things down. 'Did you hear that, Melanie? Latest reports tell us that this wild beast of Beech Hill is not, repeat NOT, a wolf!'

'Not a wolf?' Someone in the huddle of excited onlookers sounded disappointed.

'A wild dog then?'

'It still sounds vicious and nasty to me.'

'*I* certainly wouldn't want to meet it up a dark

32

alley.' There was a murmur of comments as the bunch of disgruntled people went back to their seats.

'What do you think we should do?' Bonnie Simms turned to Paul for advice. 'A lot of us are worried about our own pets. We know what it can do to a tough little dog like a Jack Russell. My poor cats wouldn't stand a chance!'

Carly noticed the way Mrs Simms lowered her voice and swivelled her eyes when she spoke to her dad. It was plain that she valued his opinion above everyone else's. Of course, she would look up to him because of what he'd done for Cleo. Still, the way she took him to one side for a private talk made Carly feel hot and uncomfortable. She saw Mel nudge Bupinda with her elbow, then both women raised their eyebrows and smiled.

'Isn't there anybody here who can tell me about my dog?' a loud voice suddenly demanded.

An old man stood glaring round reception, dog-lead in hand. His jacket was shabby, his face unshaven.

'I had a message to come here and collect him!'

He shuffled towards the desk, peering short-sightedly.

'Mr Price?' Bupinda asked.

'That's me. You've got Russ. When can I take him home?'

Carly's dad stepped forward. 'Come this way, Mr Price, and we'll tell you all about it.' He signalled for Carly to follow them into one of the treatment rooms. A buzz of gossip had started up again as people realised who the old man was.

So she shut the door on the crowd and stood by as her dad described Russ's injuries.

The old man squinted through narrowed eyes. 'He's pretty bad, then?'

'Serious but stable.'

Carly fetched a chair for Mr Price and helped him to sit down.

'But he's going to be all right, isn't he?' The gruff voice had faded to a wheezy whisper.

'It's too early to say. The operation went smoothly and Russ came round from the anaesthetic just a few minutes ago. Would you like to see him?'

Mr Price nodded. 'Last night in the park, I only

turned my back for a minute, then he was gone,' he protested. 'There's no one like Russ for doing as he's told as a rule. Steady as a rock, never any trouble.' He sighed, as he followed Carly and Paul into the intensive care unit.

'I'm sure he isn't,' Paul Grey agreed. 'He's a tough little chap, isn't he?'

'He is that.' Mr Price looked lost amongst all the machines and monitors. 'I called him time and time again, but he never came back. I couldn't understand it at all.'

'Now, Mr Price, Russ has had a rough time of it, so you must be prepared for what you see.' Paul Grey laid a hand on the old man's arm. 'Are you sure you're up to it?'

He nodded. 'Russ needs to know I'm here, doesn't he?'

'It'll certainly help pull him through. Are you ready?'

Carly held her breath as her father led the old man to Russ's unit. The cage was open at the front, with tubes hanging from stands, dripping fluid through a needle inserted into the dog's front leg. Russ lay with his head resting on the floor, his poor face stitched and bandaged.

'Eh, Russ, you've been in the wars, haven't you?' His owner's voice cracked and broke as he leaned forward to gaze at him.

'It probably looks worse than it is,' Paul Grey promised. 'It was touch and go until we gave him a transfusion to replace the blood he'd lost in the fight. But once we'd got him over the shock and seen him through the night, his chances went up considerably.'

Mr Price shook his head. 'A fight, you say? Something made a proper mess of the old boy!'

'Unfortunately we don't know what yet. You didn't see anything at the time?'

'No. Like I say, I looked away, and when I turned back there was no sign of him. I went up and down that park looking for him, calling his name until well after dark.'

'Which side of the park?' Carly asked. It was big, and split into two by the long, narrow lake.

'By the football pavilion, where I always walk him.'

'He was found by the council stores, at the far side of the park.'

Russ's owner stooped to stroke him. The dog's eyes had latched on to him and followed every movement. His ears twitched and he whined as Mr Price touched his sore head. 'Sorry, boy!' He withdrew his hand.

'It happened just as it was getting dark, and my eyesight's not what it used to be,' he confessed. 'I never looked on this side of the lake. At one point I thought he might have gone home without me, so I trudged back there. Then, when he wasn't at the house, I went back to the park looking for him one more time. I didn't get back finally until after midnight. I went to bed shattered, slept through and got up, ready to start looking again this morning. Then your secretary rang me up and told me what had happened.'

'Luckily someone brought him to the Rescue Centre for you,' Paul Grey told him. 'A local boy, Jon Hood – lives just down the road on Beacon Street.'

The name sounded odd when her dad gave the old man the official version. Carly only ever thought of him as Hoody. She felt a twinge of guilt, remembering how she'd upset him.

'And he saved Russ's life, you reckon?' Mr Price took a deep breath. 'So what'll happen now, Mr . . . ?'

'Grey. Paul Grey. Now we have to keep our fingers crossed and hope that the jaw will knit itself back together. We'll keep Russ in and feed him intravenously – by liquid through these special tubes.'

'How much will it cost?' He shook his head and looked away from the dog to the drawn blinds across the window.

'We won't talk about that just now. I'm sure we can work something out, so there's no need to worry. The main thing is to make sure that Russ is well looked after.'

'So I can't take him home?' Mr Price took the lead from his pocket and held it up.

Carly's dad smiled. 'Not just yet, I'm afraid.'

'You hear that, Russ?' His owner stood up. 'You have to stay here until you're better.'

The dog whined as he saw Mr Price shove the lead back into his pocket.

'I know, lad. It's not fair, is it?' Once more his voice broke. Then he sniffed and pulled himself back together. 'But it won't be for long, you hear? You get yourself back on your feet, and the minute they say you're fit to come home. I'll be here to collect you!'

'That's the spirit!' Paul helped him to the door. 'But to be honest, Mr Price, Russ isn't in any condition to be thinking about going home yet. Give us a few more days.'

He nodded, took one last look at his dog and shuffled out.

Carly followed. 'You can come and see him whenever you want,' she told him.

The old man sighed and blew through his cheeks. 'It breaks my heart to see him like that,' he confessed. 'Normally there's no stopping him. He's a live wire is Russ.'

'Whenever you feel like it,' Carly said again, showing him through the waiting room towards the main door.

But before he made it to the exit, a busybody in the queue stepped in their way. She held the newspaper under the old man's nose. 'Is yours the little dog that got hurt?'

'That's him.' Mr Price took the paper and

squinted at it. 'I haven't got my glasses with me. What's it say?'

'It says there's a killer on the loose in the park.' The stranger enjoyed filling in a few details. 'Some kind of wolf-dog. That's what had a go at your Jack Russell!'

'And did they find it?' Mr Price asked.

Carly noticed his hand was trembling as he spoke.

'Not yet.' The woman shook her head. 'It got away without a trace. And now none of our pets are safe. I for one won't let my Sable go near the park until that terrible thing is caught!' She clutched her pure-black cat to her chest protectively.

'The sooner they find it the better,' someone else agreed from the bench by the window.

'They should shoot it on sight!' another voice chipped in. 'No questions asked!'

'Quite right!'

'Here comes the inspector now!' Bonnie Simms was the first to see the van reappear in the car-park.

As old Mr Price slipped quietly away, the rest

waited anxiously, ready to hang on Steve's every word.

'Did you see Sharon? What did she say?' Mel asked.

'Hang on, let me catch my breath.' He'd hardly had a chance to step through the door. Flinging his cap on to Bupinda's desk, he told them that he'd been to visit Mel's friend, Sharon Charlton, and she'd been able to confirm that she'd actually seen the creature with her own eyes.

'So what was it? Could she say?' Mel was excited all over again by the idea that she might have given Steve the vital clue.

Steve shook his head. 'Sorry, Mel. You'll have to wait till I've made a proper report.'

A groan went round the room.

'It's confidential information.' He spread his hands, palms upwards, then spotted Carly waiting quietly to one side. 'How about putting the kettle on for a cup of coffee?'

She nodded and went straight to the office, setting out Steve's mug, waiting for the water to boil. The way rumours were flying around, she had begun to feel her head spin. Now she was glad of a few minutes' peace as the kettle hummed and she looked out at the bright blue sky.

Steve soon followed her. He sat at the desk and took the steaming mug from her, leaning back in his chair. 'Don't look at me like that!' he warned.

'Like what?' She hadn't said a word.

'With those big brown eyes. I'm not supposed to give anything away just yet; you know that.'

'I never said you should.' Carly retreated to the window.

'You gave me that look.' Steve grinned and relented. 'OK, keep it quiet, but I saw Sharon Charlton and she gave a pretty good description of the animal that was attacking the stray dog. She said it was big, but not that big. So it could have been another dog after all. She told me that things had got out of hand when she told people about it at the time of the attack. Suddenly this animal got to be huge, like the Hound of the Baskervilles!'

'I know.' Carly saw how it could happen. 'Did she say what kind of dog?'

Steve sighed. 'She wasn't sure. It sounded like a long-haired German shepherd to me.'

'But they're black and brown! I thought she said it was grey?'

'She reckons it could have been the mist. She wasn't very sure about anything, when it came to it.' Steve sounded weary as he sipped his coffee.

'So what did you do next?'

'Came away, made a few phone calls. You're not going to like this, Carly, but I got reports that a stray German shepherd *has* been spotted on and off.'

'Where? When?' Suddenly she fired up. Surely Steve couldn't be saying that a beautiful German shepherd dog could turn out to be the Beast of Beech Hill?

'It's not been seen much in the park, it's true . . .'

'Well then!' Now her eyes flashed and she tossed her wavy dark hair back from her face.

'It's mainly on that industrial wasteland near Sharon Charlton's office, behind the Morningside Estate. Do you know it?'

Carly nodded. 'By Fiveways and the King Edward's Road allotments. But since when?'

'Since before the first unexplained attack up

there in June.' Just then the office door creaked and Steve glanced up. 'That's odd. I thought I'd shut that properly.'

Carly went to close the door. 'It still doesn't prove anything, just because there's a stray dog loose. There are always stray dogs. We bring them to the Rescue Centre all the time! That doesn't mean they're all vicious killers!' She would stick up for any dog unlucky enough to attract this sort of wild rumour.

'That's true,' Steve admitted. 'You're right, I won't jump to any conclusions.' He drew a form out of the drawer, ready to write his report. 'Close that door, will you?'

But Carly found that it wouldn't shut. As she pushed, someone shoved from the other side.

'It's only us.' Bonnie Simms's head appeared in the crack. She came into the room, followed by Carly's dad. 'Did you hear that?' she asked, a note of tension in her voice. 'I'm sorry, Steve, but we couldn't help overhearing. You say it's a stray German shepherd we're after?'

'I don't think he did say that,' Paul Grey pointed out.

'But it makes perfect sense!' Mrs Simms was the sort of woman who seized on a whisper of an idea and made it into absolute proof. 'It would be the right size and shape. People often say that German shepherds look like wolves. It would be an understandable mistake to make if you were panicking, wouldn't it?' She waved away all objections. 'What's happened is that this stray dog has turned feral, reverted to its original hunting instincts!'

'Maybe, maybe not.' Paul Grey wouldn't be rushed into hasty conclusions.

'Oh come on, this stray dog and the mystery attacker are one and the same animal, and you know it!' She raced on. 'We've no time to lose. It could attack again!'

'What do you suggest?' Steve stood up and strode angrily across the room. He stood beside Carly at the window.

'It's obvious.' She was one hundred per cent, cast-iron certain about what they should do. 'Call the police. Describe this dog to them. Get them to bring it in here and put it to sleep straight away!'

4

Carly steadied her nerves to help in the surgery for the rest of that day. Doing practical jobs calmed her down, and she knew that despite what Bonnie Simms had said, it would take a while before the overworked police force got on to the case of a stray German shepherd. They had a bit of time to decide what to do.

'Did she actually phone the police?' Liz asked. A pretty little Yorkshire terrier sat patiently on the treatment table, her long, silky hair shining in a shaft of sunlight. The vet examined a small lesion on the inside of her nose, while the anxious owner stood nearby.

'Yep. You know what she's like. She rang from here.' Carly stroked the dog. 'Good girl, Donna. It won't be long now.'

'Mrs Parsons, I'm taking a biopsy,' Liz explained. 'I think Donna may be suffering from something called an auto-immunity problem.'

The dog's owner frowned. 'Is it serious?'

'It could be if we don't treat it. But don't worry, you've brought her along in good time. Once we're sure about what it is, we can begin treatment.' She smiled and told Carly to hand the trembling little dog back to the woman. 'I'll give you a ring as soon as we get the results from the lab.'

As Carly showed them out, she checked the next patient on the list. It was a tabby cat called Tiger for her dad to examine in treatment room number one. In came a mother and daughter with Tiger safely inside a sealed box.

Paul Grey waited for Carly to lift the cat from the box. 'Any news from the police?' he asked. The problem preyed on everyone's minds.

'Not so far.' She settled Tiger on the table and smiled at the little girl. 'He'll be fine,' she promised, as the mother took her daughter to wait in reception.

'Dad . . .' Carly waited until he'd finished examining the cat's inflamed third eyelid. 'You know what Mrs Simms said about the stray dog's hunting instinct coming out again?'

'Yep. I said I wasn't certain about that.'

'Why not?' Carly wanted to be sure of her facts.

'Because a German shepherd wasn't bred for hunting, like a fox-terrier, say. A terrier still has a strong urge to chase and kill a quarry. But a German shepherd is what its name suggests: a herding dog. By nature it wouldn't be likely to go out and kill.'

'Is that why you don't think the animal in the park is the stray German shepherd?'

He nodded and prescribed antibiotics for Tiger's eye infection. 'He'll soon be as good as new,' he called through to the little girl. 'Anyone else?' he asked Carly, as the patient and his owners thanked him and left.

'No, Tiger was the last.' She wiped down the

table, then looked at her watch. 'Is it OK if I go and find Hoody?'

'I thought you two had a row?' Paul Grey took off his white coat and hung it on a peg.

'We did. I want to say sorry.' She blushed.

'Wow, this must be a first!' her dad kidded. 'Shall I contact the *Guinness Book of Records*?'

'Ha-ha. Anyway, I need his help.'

'To do what?' He followed her into reception, where Bupinda and Mel were also packing up for the day.

'Nothing. It's not important.' She tried to sound light and casual, in case Hoody should turn round and say no.

'Anything to do with a certain German shepherd, by any chance?' Her dad could always read her thoughts.

She tossed her head and turned away.

'Hey, Carly, no!' Mel heard the words 'German shepherd'. 'You're not thinking of going near that thing, are you? It's a killer, remember!'

'Who says?' Carly put on her stubborn face. She pursed her lips and tilted her head back. 'Has anyone actually proved that he's guilty?'

'No, but the police are taking it seriously. They took Bonnie Simms's word for it and they're looking for him right now.'

'All the more reason!' Carly insisted. The stories didn't scare her. She just wanted to get to the poor dog and check him out before anyone else did.

'It's the police's job. I'd leave it to them if I were you.' Bupinda sided with Mel. 'The dog is probably very dangerous!'

The receptionist and the nurse turned to Paul. 'You're not going to let her risk her own safety, are you?' Mel demanded.

But Carly was already swinging through the door. 'It's OK, I know what I'm doing!'

'Stop her!' Mel insisted.

'How?' Paul Grey knew what Carly was like. All he could do was follow her outside and take her by the arm to make her listen for a few moments before she went off to find Hoody. 'Look, Carly, I know we don't think it's likely that this dog is the real culprit, and I do trust you to know what you're doing.'

She smiled briefly then nodded.

'But don't put yourself in any danger, OK?' His

grey eyes held hers. Then he released her arm and let her go on her way. 'Just remember, no big, pointless heroics!'

The city streets were bathed in warm evening light. Long shadows fell across lawns and pavements, there was a smell of hot tarmac, petrol fumes, food from the shops and cafes on City Road.

'Have you seen Hoody?' Carly asked a group of kids standing at the corner of Hillman's supermarket.

'Yeah,' one girl replied.

'Where?'

'Down the park.'

Carly turned to retrace her steps.

'That was last night, stupid!' someone else pointed out, to save Carly the bother.

'Well, she never asked *when*, did she?' The girl giggled, then walked off.

'So, has anyone seen him lately?' Carly scuffed her shoe against the kerb and tried not to sound too keen.

'Why, what's he done?'

'Nothing. I just want to talk to him.'

'Oo-ooh!'

'Somebody had better tell him to look out!'

The gang did their best to make her squirm.

'Yeah, yeah!' They could tease all they liked; she didn't care. The reason she had to find Hoody was important. 'So you haven't seen him?'

'I have.' A smaller girl at the back of the crowd decided to help. 'He was down on Morningside with Vinny.'

Carly knew the estate of tower blocks well. 'Great. Thanks, Harmony.' She could cut down a back road to Beacon Street, then across to Morningside.

'Watch it, he was in a bad mood!' The older kids were still bent on making life difficult. They drifted across the pavement after Carly.

'Hoody, in a bad mood? Never!'

'How can you tell?'

'If he wasn't in a bad mood before, he will be when *you* find him!' they called after her.

She ignored them and slipped across the road before the lights changed. OK, so Hoody wasn't going to be pleased to see her, not after this

52

morning. But she needed an ally. She ran down a hill lined with small terraced houses, then across a road into the estate. Where now? Morningside was huge. It had six tall blocks of flats that hardly anyone wanted to live in. Many were boarded up and sprayed with graffiti.

Carly slowed down by the entrance to one of the tower blocks. She drew breath and looked all around. A few women pushed kids in push-chairs laden with shopping across the footpaths between the blocks. A boy on a bike had built a ramp out of bricks and planks of wood.

'Have you seen Hoody?' she yelled.

He rode up the ramp and shook his head. 'Try his house!'

'He's never in!' she called back. 'There's no point.' Hoody might as well have no home, the amount of time he spent there with his sister, Zoe, and her boyfriend. So she went on through the estate, still looking.

In the end, she was yelling his name down side alleys and up at the balconies of the boarded-up flats. It was getting late. The sun had gone down and everywhere was in shadow. If she didn't find him soon she would have to try to find the stray dog alone. It could be a dangerous decision, though, and she'd promised her dad that she would be careful.

'Hoody!' Her voice echoed along an empty balcony. She'd climbed a couple of floors to get a better view of the estate. '-*Oody-oody-oody!*' her voice came back.

There was a bark from down below, then she saw a flash of brown and black dog come hurtling up the concrete steps.

'Vinny!' Her face lit up as he cannoned along the balcony. The dog skidded to a halt and waited to be stroked. 'Where have you been? I've been looking all over for you!'

Slowly Hoody came into view on a patch of scrubby grass below. 'What do you want?' He stood hands in pockets, head on one side, looking up at her.

Carly swallowed hard and framed the difficult sentence. 'I wanted to say sorry.'

'So? What do you want?' His expression stayed the same: blank.

'Come on, Vinny.' She led him along the

balcony, down the steps. 'How long have you been hanging around?' she asked Hoody when she reached the patch of grass. 'Didn't you hear me shouting for you?'

He shrugged. 'You still haven't told me what you want.'

'Are you still mad at me?'

'Who says I'm mad?'

'You always answer a question with a question when you're mad.'

'Do I?'

'See!' She broke into a grin. 'I really am sorry for getting at you this morning. And I'd be really, really glad if you stopped sulking now!'

'Why should I?' The blank stare didn't shift.

'Because I need your help.' This was called swallowing her pride. It stuck in her throat and made the words come out strange and strangled.

'What sort of help?' Questions bristled out of him as he turned away and began to walk off.

'With this wild-dog problem. I want you to help me find it before the police!'

'You could be too late.' He threw the remark over his shoulder, going off at a lope, shoulders hunched, hands still deep in his jeans pockets. 'Their van has been cruising round the place all afternoon.'

Carly knew that this must be true. Hoody always knew everything that was going on in the area. 'But they haven't found him yet?' She ran alongside. 'Listen, Hoody, if the police do find the dog, you know they'll have him put down?'

'Yep. You should hear the people round here. Everyone's going on about it. They're saying it'll go for a little kid next. All the mothers are going spare.'

'Do you believe them?' She put on a spurt of speed and stood across his path. 'Do you, Hoody?'

'What's it matter if I believe them or not? That Mrs Simms has got her own search party together. It's a bunch of mad mothers and pet owners, all saying they think the dog should be shot on sight.'

'No!' This was news to Carly. Again, she trusted Hoody's word. 'So, there's the police van and another group? Listen, this dog doesn't stand a chance if we don't get to it first!'

' "We"?' He tried to sidestep out of her way.

She darted after him. 'Come on, Hoody! You know the places round here better than anyone. You and Vinny could find this dog, no problem!'

He looked at her and chewed his lip. 'If we wanted to, yeah.'

'So, what? You're going to do nothing and let him die just because you're still sulking?' Carly pleaded one last time. 'Because he will die, one way or another, unless we get to him and prove that he's not the one! They'll say he's the killer, whether he is or not! They'll put him down.'

Hoody narrowed his eyes. '*If* they find him.'

'Hoody, do you know something?' It was the way he said 'if' that made her ask.

'I know they're looking in all the wrong places.' Behind his shoulder, the last shade of pink tinged the clear sky. Soon the estate would fall into darkness.

'How do you know that? Do you know where this dog is?'

'Maybe.'

'Where? Where is he?' Hoody was driving her mad. Her voice rose, she started to look in all the shadowy places under the tower blocks, through the tunnel underpasses.

'This way,' he said, maddeningly calm. He led her off down one of the underpasses towards the empty factories and wasteland beyond. 'He's made a kind of den in the middle of a tip. It's not far from here. Vinny tracked him down. Good boy, Vin. Let's go!'

The dog *was* pure German shepherd. He crouched amongst empty oil barrels and piles of rubble in what must have been an old factory yard. There were tall brick walls on every side, dark shadows everywhere. At first, all Carly could see was the stray creature's eyes glittering in the dark.

'Careful!' Hoody warned her not to go too near.

The dog bared his fangs and growled. He didn't shift from his den. Instead, the black hair at the scruff of his neck stood on end, and the growl became a snarl.

'There's something wrong with him!' Carly gasped. Any healthy dog would have come out and stood his ground. 'Look at him: he's too weak to stand up!' She could make out his skinny sides, with the ribs sticking out. His mane of brown hair was matted and tangled.

'Don't risk it!' Hoody saw her take a step forward. 'Look at Vinny. He's decided to stay back.'

Hoody's dog had taken up a low, crouching position nearby.

'What are we going to do?' Carly whispered. 'He's sick. We can't leave him here!'

As she spoke, the dog seemed to gather his strength. He managed to stand up to his full height, more than seventy centimetres tall, still snarling out his warning at the strangers. But when he tried to move, one front leg collapsed under him. He stumbled and fell to the ground.

'Poor thing!' She ignored Hoody's warning and rushed forward. Keeping clear of the dog's snarling jaws, she caught a look at what was bothering him. The paw on the front leg was badly swollen and covered in blood from an old wound.

But then he was staggering to his feet and warning her away from his den, growling at her from deep in his throat. His teeth flashed white in the darkness, his jaws snapped.

Scared for him, full of dread over what would happen if anyone else discovered his derelict hiding-place, Carly took a few steps back. From a safe distance, she watched the dog sink to the ground once more.

'We'd better leave him.' Hoody knew they couldn't move the injured dog by themselves. 'Come on, Carly, let's get out of here.' He was afraid someone would hear them, that they would give the dog away.

She nodded. But she backed away, unable to take her eyes off the suffering animal. 'You know what this means?' she whispered. There was one good thing in the terrible scene they'd just come across. The dog lay panting and exhausted, watching them retreat.

'It means we've got one sick animal to rescue, and don't ask me how!' Hoody had hold of Vinny and was making him back off out of the old yard.

'But something good as well.' They reached the broken-down entrance, stood amongst tall weeds and overgrown grass. She took a deep breath and turned to Hoody. 'It means this poor dog can't possibly be the killer that's loose in Beech Hill Park!'

5

'Nothing so far.' A young policeman leaned his elbows on Bupinda's desk and answered Mel's eager inquiry. 'We were out in the van until dusk yesterday evening, but we didn't see hide nor hair of the beast.'

It was early the next morning and Carly had had another restless night. Her mind was filled with pictures of the thin, shivering dog holed up in the old factory yard.

'Maybe you were looking in the wrong places,' Mel said, sneaking a look at Carly.

Carly and Hoody hadn't said a word to anybody about what they'd found.

'Who can we tell?' she'd whispered the night
before, as they'd stood outside the Rescue Centre
in the pitch-dark, trying to decide what to do.

'Your dad?' He'd done one of his shrugs,
challenging her to come up with a better idea.

'I don't think so.' Though she longed to tell
him, she knew they would only be putting him
in an impossible position. If Paul Grey knew
where the supposedly vicious dog was hiding,
he would be bound to tell the police, she knew.

'What, then?'

'We'd better keep it a secret for now,' she said
at last. 'Between you and me, OK?'

He'd nodded abruptly and turned on his heel.
'I might go and take another look first thing
tomorrow,' he'd muttered.

'Don't let anyone see you!'

Hoody had tutted and walked off. *Do me a
favour*.

Now Carly coloured up under Mel's sus-
picious glance. The policeman, too, was looking
curiously at her.

'We concentrated on the area around the park,' he told them. He was tall and fair-haired, with broad shoulders and an open, friendly face. 'But to be honest, there were so many people out there that there was no chance of this so-called killer animal putting in an appearance. It seems that everybody and his aunt has read the newspaper article. And you know what it's like: give most people a whiff of drama and they'll come creeping out of the woodwork to take a look.'

'Didn't they know they were getting in your way?' Mel asked.

'No. They probably mean well, forming search parties of their own, that sort of thing. We issued a warning that it might be dangerous, but it didn't make any difference.' The policeman turned to Steve, who had come out of the office to talk to him. 'Have you picked up anything else useful from those case notes?'

'Not a lot. Here's the name and number of the woman whose dog was attacked last month.' Steve handed over a piece of paper. 'I went to see Sharon Charlton at Fiveways yesterday. She's the one who saw this monster beast lay into a stray dog up there. It turns out it wasn't so much a monster – more likely another stray. A German shepherd by the sound of it.'

While the men talked, Carly kept her face hidden in a stack of letters and leaflets that had just arrived in the post. She went to stick a leaflet on the notice-board to do with banning the use of monkeys in scientific research and testing.

The policeman took the piece of paper with Sharon's name and number. 'Maybe we should shift our search over in that direction?'

Steve nodded. 'It's possible that this creature, whatever it is, comes on forays into the park but lives somewhere else. The old industrial estate would certainly be more isolated these days; a safer bet for him to make a hide-away.' Steve saw the sense of him coming to the park every now and then for easy pickings.

Carly kept her back turned, pressing drawing-pins into the board. What could she say? If she tried to warn the policeman off, she would only attract suspicion.

'OK, we'll do that then.' He picked up his hat from the desk and put it on. Then he made a confession to Steve. 'I'll tell you what, I'll be glad when we find the thing and people can relax.'

'I know what you mean.' It wasn't part of an inspector's job that Steve enjoyed: tracking down and destroying dangerous animals.

'As it is, there's a big panic. We keep getting phone calls at the station to say there's been another sighting. First it's a huge black cat, then it's an even more enormous grey creature shaped like a wolf. Before long we'll be getting calls to say they've seen a lion on the loose! It's amazing what they'll say when panic sets in like this.'

Steve nodded and showed him out. But the door had hardly swung to when Carly saw Bonnie Simms running barefoot across the carpark, her face drained of colour, her cardigan flapping open.

She burst into the surgery, crying out for help. 'Get someone quickly, before it's too late!'

Paul and Liz both came running. Mel moved forward to stop Bonnie from stumbling, then she took something from her.

'It's a cat, unconscious, losing a lot of blood!' Mel said, looking up in alarm.

'It's Rameses!' Bonnie cried. 'He's been attacked. I found him like this at the bottom of the garden!'

'Take him through.' Paul Grey swung into action. He asked Carly to clean up the pool of blood that had trickled on to the floor, then follow them into the operating theatre. 'We'll need to resuscitate him pretty fast,' he told her. 'We need all hands on deck for this one.'

'But he's going to be all right?' Rameses' owner pleaded. Her white shirt was stained red. 'He's not going to die?'

'We hope not. We'll do everything we can,' Paul told her, before he vanished into the operating theatre.

Bonnie turned to Carly. 'Oh, help him! Please help him!'

Carly stooped to wipe up the stain of blood from the floor. She noticed the policeman and Steve heading back inside, and Bupinda arriving for the start of morning surgery. Relieved, she handed over the distressed owner to them.

Then she hurried to help her father, Liz and Mel.

The injured cat lay, still unconscious, on the operating table. He was a long, sleek grey cat, like Cleopatra, but there was an open wound on his neck and his thick coat was matted with blood. Liz stood poised with an oxygen mask, while Carly's dad tried to stop the flow of fresh blood.

'Looks like the major artery has been severed,' he muttered. He tried to pick up a heartbeat with his stethoscope, then shook his head.

Liz stepped back and hooked the oxygen mask back in place. Mel wheeled the resuscitation trolley away.

'Try, Dad!' Carly begged. Bonnie Simms's pleas were still fresh in her ears. Rameses lay quite still, his eyes closed, head tilted back, legs stretched straight out.

'No point,' Paul told her gently. 'The poor cat's stopped breathing, there's no heartbeat. He's dead, Carly.' It was final.

For a moment she refused to believe it. Yes, the cat was badly injured. But her father was the best vet around. Surely he could fight to save Rameses? She moved in to plead with him once more.

But Liz put a hand on her shoulder and turned her away from the operating table. 'It was probably already too late when Mrs Simms brought him in. We couldn't find any vital signs. There was nothing we could do.'

Carly stared at her through tear-filled eyes. 'Are you sure?'

'Believe me.' Liz hugged her and led her gently away.

'I saw it with my own eyes!'

'Steady on!'

'I did! I was walking through the park, on my way here to visit Russ. Clear as day, I saw what happened!' Old Mr Price was almost shouting into the young policeman's face.

'Slow down. Take it easy.'

Carly had come out of the operating theatre in a daze. Now here in reception there was another uproar.

'Take Bonnie into a treatment room,' Liz told Bupinda.

'I want to see Paul! Where is he? I must speak to him!' Mrs Simms hardly seemed to understand that her cat was dead. She looked over her shoulder as the receptionist guided her away.

'I'm here.' Carly's father took off his stained gloves and gown as he swung through the doors out of theatre. 'It's OK,' he told Liz, 'I'll explain exactly what happened. Bring us a cup of tea, would you, Carly?'

The cat's death had knocked her sideways into confusion, but she grasped on to the practical job: make a cup of tea. As she boiled the kettle and set out a mug, she listened to Mr Price's angry accusations.

'I tell you, I was on the spot. There was no one else in the park, not at this time of the morning. I was going along, minding my own business, when I heard this terrible row start up in some bushes at the back of a garden.'

'Where exactly?' The policeman managed to slip in a question.

'A big house just up the road from here.'

'That would be Mrs Simms's place,' Mel confirmed. 'What kind of noise, Mr Price?'

'Snarling and snapping. Something big and nasty. I knew straight away what it was.' The old man gave his account in a strong voice, but his hands were trembling, Carly noticed. 'It had to be this mystery beast, didn't it? And there it was, a nasty brute. Big and powerful. The poor cat never stood a chance.'

'What sort of animal was it, Mr Price?' The policeman asked steadily. 'Was it a dog?'

The old man hesitated. 'I didn't get right up to it. I kept my distance, otherwise it might have turned on me.'

'Quite right.'

'But I could see it well enough. And I could hear the savage brute.'

All eyes were turned on the old man, who stood in the middle of the waiting area, his fists clenched now, his shoulders hunched.

'Could you identify what sort of dog it was?' The policeman was as patient as ever.

'Easy. Long hair, mostly brown with a bit of black, long, bushy tail. I got a good view of it when it went sloping off across the park after the attack. I knew straight away what sort of dog I was looking at. It was a German shepherd, without a shadow of a doubt.'

71

*

'What more proof do we need?' Bonnie Simms had drunk a cup of tea and was recovering from the shock of her cat's death.

Paul Grey had asked her to sign a form. 'If you give us permission, we'll be able to send the body to the Vet Investigation Unit for a post-mortem examination,' he explained.

'But we know who the killer is!' She burst into tears as she spoke. 'I don't see the point.'

'Perhaps we need evidence which is a bit more scientific than one eye-witness report,' he pointed out as gently as he could.

'What sort of evidence?' Her eyes were dark and doubtful. She shuddered at what the vet was asking.

'I suppose you might call it forensic clues to back up Mr Price's evidence.'

'Such as?' She insisted on knowing.

'Well, a scientist at the Unit would study the major wound inflicted by this attacker. He or she would be able to tell a lot from the depth of the wound, its width, the angle it was made from, and so on.'

'How horrible,' Bonnie Simms whispered.

Carly waited in the treatment room after she'd handed over the tea. She watched the careful way her dad handled the distressed owner. She knew that Mrs Simms trusted him.

'It would give the police a lot of help,' he told her. 'Our inspector, Steve Winter, would drive Rameses across town and bring him back for us to carry out your wishes as far as the body is concerned. Meanwhile, the police would continue looking for a dog that fits the description given by Mr Price. Between the two of you, we should be one hundred per cent sure that we've got the right animal.'

He sounded so calm, so certain, that at last Bonnie Simms gave her permission.

'Is it all right if I stay here for a while?' she asked, after she'd signed the form. 'I'd like to be with Cleo and the kittens.'

'That's fine.' He smiled and nodded. 'Carly will take you up to see them. She could show you how to hand-feed the kittens through a dropper until Cleo is strong enough to take over.'

Bonnie sniffed and squared her shoulders. 'Thanks, Paul.'

'Before you know it, you'll be taking them all home. You won't be able to move in the house for kittens getting into mischief!' He persuaded her to look forward rather than back.

Carly led her up the stairs. In their special unit, the kittens were awake and hungry, so she prepared the milk straight away. Meanwhile, Bonnie took Cleo in her arms and gently stroked her. The cat purred loudly.

'There, Cleo, there!' she murmured, putting her face against the cat's soft fur. 'Everything's going to be all right. We'll soon have you home. And the horrible dog will be caught, and there'll be no more danger!' Her voice trembled and fresh tears threatened to spill down her cheeks.

'Have you thought of names for the kittens yet?' Carly changed the subject. She took up the smallest one first and began to give her the feed. The kitten gulped it down.

'Not yet.' She couldn't help sighing as she put Cleo back in her cage. 'I was going to do that today, but now it doesn't feel like the right time somehow.' In spite of her sadness she smiled at the greedy little kitten. 'Here, let me have a go.'

Carly offered her the dropper and the kitten. 'She might seem tiny and helpless, but there's no need to worry. She's tougher than she looks,' she told her.

Soon, Bonnie had the kitten nestled in her hand, busily feeding once more.

'Can you manage?' Carly wanted to nip downstairs to check what was happening . Recent events had been a disaster, not only for Rameses and Bonnie Simms, but for the chief suspect as well. Now Mr Price had positively identified a German shepherd as the savage beast of Beech Hill, it meant that time was running out for the dog hiding out in the factory yard. She urgently needed to contact Hoody and ask him what they should do next.

'Yes, you go.' Mrs Simms had settled into the task. 'It's nice and peaceful here. I'll enjoy this job.'

Carly went out and took the stairs two at a time. 'Where's Steve?' she asked Bupinda, scanning the queue of morning patients.

'Gone to the VIU to get a post-mortem done on that poor cat.'

She nodded. 'What about the policeman?'

'Out looking for the culprit.' Bupinda sent a patient into treatment room number one. 'Why?'

'Nothing. It doesn't matter. Where's Dad?'

'In the other treatment room. Honestly, Carly, would you just calm down for a second?' The receptionist fended off more questions. She was busy with her list.

So Carly shot off to find him, catching him between patients.

He looked up when she opened the door. 'Pity about poor old Rameses.'

She nodded. 'Dad, about last night . . .' She paused. 'About Hoody and me and the stray dog . . .'

'Shh!' He held up a hand to interrupt. 'You notice I never asked, and I did that on purpose. You don't have to tell me if you don't want to.'

'I do and I don't.'

'Carly, think before you say any more. If you tell me something that I think the police should know, I won't be able to keep it from them!'

She realised in a flash that he'd worked the whole thing out for himself, and that he trusted her judgement. 'What if I'm wrong?' she asked breathlessly.

'If you're wrong and the rest of the people round here are right – if this German shepherd really is the killer – then it's serious,' he admitted. He never built things up or exaggerated.

Slowly she nodded. 'He'll kill again, won't he?'

'Probably.' He looked her in the eye. 'You don't think you're wrong, do you?'

Carly held his gaze. This was one of the biggest decisions of her life. 'No! I think the dog's innocent. I can't tell you why, but I'm practically sure he isn't the one!'

It was Paul Grey's turn to nod his head; just once. 'Me, too,' he said quietly, as his next patient came into the room and the surgery continued.

6

It wasn't hard for Carly to find Hoody. He was hanging out with Vinny in the park as usual, messing about on the swings meant for the younger kids. It was gone ten, and though it was the school holidays most parents had kept their children out of the park until the mystery attacker was caught.

'It's like a ghost town.' Hoody saw her and swung an empty swing high into the air. Its chains slackened and rattled before the swing came plunging back. He caught it and swung it again.

'Everyone's scared stiff. I don't suppose you can blame them. Even I've decided to keep Ruby indoors until the mystery's solved.' Carly sat quietly on a nearby roundabout, giving it a shove with one foot. It turned slowly. 'Did you hear about Mrs Simms's tomcat?'

'Yep. The whole world heard about it.'

'She's upset. And you know that Mr Price blamed the German shepherd?' Carly watched the swing arc into the air once more. The chain clattered against the crossbar, then the seat dipped to the ground.

'Yep. But he's wrong about that.' Hoody left off messing and came to stand near the roundabout. He gave it a hefty shove to send it spinning faster. 'It couldn't have been the German shepherd.'

Carly clung on to a nearby bar. 'I know that. But we need proof.' She told him about the Investigation Unit and Steve's trip across town to get the evidence they wanted. It was weird trying to talk to him as she spun on the roundabout: she caught glimpses of his pale face and cropped brown hair, then there would be a whirl of trees and grass until he came back into view.

'Waste of time.' He snorted and turned his back. 'And time is what we haven't got, remember!'

'Hoody, hang on!' She crept to the edge of the spinning roundabout, ready to jump off and follow him. 'What do you mean, the post-mortem is a waste of time?' She leaped and landed on the grass. She'd come to the park to find him, to ask him what they should do next, not risk breaking her leg on the stupid roundabout. She was angry as she followed him towards the soccer pavilion.

'There's no need for it. I could tell them it wasn't the German shepherd.'

'Because of his sore foot?'

'Yep. And because I was with him over in the factory yard at the exact time when he was supposed to be ripping this cat to shreds!' He was deliberately cruel: a way of showing his own frustration.

Carly gasped. For a second she wanted to run and tell everyone the news: 'The German shepherd isn't the culprit! We've got an alibi; it's something else that's doing these terrible things!'

But of course they couldn't do it without giving away his hiding-place. She was torn this way and that.

Hoody went through their choices for her. 'See? We know he's innocent, but who'd believe us? Everyone thinks the dog is guilty, and they're in a blind panic. Who'd even stop and listen to us? Especially me.' He shrugged and gave a hollow laugh. 'You: maybe. Me: no way!'

Carly took his point. 'So if we went to the police with your version of where the dog was when Rameses got killed, they'd make us lead them to him.'

'And they'd grab him, and they wouldn't listen to us, and they'd have him put down, just like that.' He clicked his fingers in disgust.

She sighed, then shuddered. 'Hoody, I've thought of something even worse!'

At Beech Hill they had a special room which Carly never went in. It wasn't much bigger than a cupboard. There was no window, only a bare table and an overhead light. This was the room where the vets took those animals too ill to treat and put them humanely to sleep.

'Are you OK?' Hoody stared at her. 'What are you shaking for?'

'Listen. Yes, the police will probably have the dog put down. They won't want to take the risk of letting him live, even if they're not one hundred per cent sure that he's the killer.' She slowed right down, speaking in a low whisper. 'And the worst thing is, once they've captured him they'll bring him to Beech Hill and get us to do the job!'

No way could they give the dog away. Hoody and Carly were both sure. He promised instead to keep an eye on the factory yard as best he could, and try to take food to the dog without drawing attention to himself and Vinny.

'And listen,' he said, his voice urgent as they walked out of the park, 'when can you meet me again?'

Once more she was torn. Part of her wanted to be on hand at the Rescue Centre, ready for Steve to come back with the post-mortem report. Part of her wanted to be out with Hoody, looking after the dog. 'About twelve,' she decided. 'Why?'

'We have to make a plan of our own.'

They stopped at the park gates. 'Like what?' Everything was running out of control. How could he talk about making plans?

'Like, finding out what really is behind these attacks. It stands to reason: if it's not our dog in the factory yard, it must be something else!'

'And you think we could find it?' Suddenly there was a straw to clutch at. 'That's a good idea. We can look at lunch-time and we might find some clues.'

'What are you on about – clues? We need to find the actual animal, don't we?'

'Yes, but think! These attacks always happen in the early morning or evening. Never in the middle of the day. This animal doesn't come out in full daylight. If we're gonna find him, we'll have to wait until it's nearly dark!' She was seeing clearly now, thanks to Hoody.

'I'll look anyway,' he insisted, crossing the road with Vinny. 'You can do what you like; wait till dark, whatever. But I'm not hanging round that long!'

She watched them go down the hill towards

Morningside: the skinny boy and his tough little dog. The funny thing was, there was Hoody complaining that no one would believe his alibi, yet Carly herself knew, in spite of their quarrels and their ups and downs, she would trust him with her life.

They got through the day. Hoody kept an eye on the stray dog, and reported back to Carly. He and Vinny combed the park for the real culprit without turning up a single clue. Like the police, the real killer had them fooled.

Meanwhile, Carly waited in vain for Steve to turn up with evidence from the post-mortem on Rameses.

'He's busy. He has a hundred and one things to do today,' Liz told her towards the end of afternoon surgery. 'For a start, he has to go up to Holybridge Bird Sanctuary. Someone phoned him on his mobile to say there was a heron entangled in some rusty wire that had been dumped in the canal. He had to rush across there to free it. Then he rang Bupinda to say he would have to take the bird straight to the sanctuary.

Then maybe after that he'll be able to call back in at the VIU for the report on Rameses.'

'What time does the Unit close?' Carly looked at her watch. It was already half past four and there was no word from Steve.

'At five.' Liz was busy checking Russ's stitches. The little terrier was recovering nicely from his ordeal, already free from the drips and tubes that had saved his life two days before. 'See how this deep wound across his nose is beginning to heal.' She showed Carly the good work the stitches had done in holding the edges of the cut together.

Russ sat patiently on the treatment table while they examined him. He was a different dog: alert now, with his brown eyes shining and following their every move.

'Of course it will take longer for the jawbone to knit back together.' Liz showed Carly how to liquidise his food and ease it between Russ's wired jaws, stroking his throat to make him swallow. 'We'll have to show Mr Price how to do this as well. It'll be a good few weeks before Russ here is tucking into a dish of chunky meat!'

'Mr Price said he'd come in to visit again later

this evening.' When Liz gave her the word, Carly lifted Russ gently from the table. 'Shall I get Bupinda to send the next one in?

Liz nodded. 'Oh, and by the way, talking of visitors . . . !' Half-smiling, she pointed to the window. 'I think those two are for you!'

Through the blind, Carly caught sight of Hoody and Vinny. They had their faces to the glass and Hoody was trying to attract her attention. He was mouthing words that she couldn't make out.

She dashed outside to meet him. 'What's happened now?'

'Nothing's happened. I think you should come and see the dog,' he told her. 'I'm worried about him.'

'Why? Have you just been over there?'

'Yep. You know how he was last night? Well, he's worse.'

'Shivering?'

'Now he can't even stand up. He just lies there whining.'

Carly had already decided to go with Hoody. They went along Beech Hill, then cut down through the park. From what he was saying, she suspected the dog must be running a high fever. 'It's probably the wound in his paw that's got infected,' she told him as they jogged with Vinny down the slope and through an avenue of tall copper-beech trees.

'What'll happen to him?'

'He should have antibiotics and plenty of fluid.' She ran through the kind of treatment the dog would get at the surgery. 'If it was really bad, we'd have to inject the antibiotics to bring the fever down as quick as we could.'

'And if not?' Hoody loped under the canopy of leaves, his face set straight ahead.

'He could die,' Carly said. There was no getting away from the fact.

Then Vinny, who had been running easily ahead, suddenly did a detour. He veered off the path and under the trees, ears pricked, picking up his feet through the long grass that grew around the silver-grey trunks of the beech trees.

Annoyed, Hoody whistled for him to come back.

But the dog ignored him. He began to sniff at the ground, then he stopped. He turned his head towards them and gave a sharp bark.

'What's he found?' Carly realised that Vinny wouldn't have run off for no reason. This was important. She decided to go and look.

Hoody followed, but he was grumbling. 'We gotta sort that dog out,' he muttered. 'We haven't got time to mess around, Vin.'

Vinny barked again. He waited for Carly to arrive, ducking his head and bouncing back up, urging her to hurry up.

'OK, let's have a look,' she told him, kneeling in the grass at his side. 'Good boy. What have you found?'

They didn't need to search far. 'Here,' Hoody muttered and pointed.

There was a squirrel lying hidden in the long grass. Carly parted the tangle of weeds and tall blades to get a better view. The poor thing was cold and stiff, its tail stretched out behind it, its front paws curled up towards its chest. 'Dead,' she said softly.

'See its face.' He showed her the familiar wounds: the torn flesh around the nose and neck. The blood had dried dark red and stained the ground. The mystery killer had struck again.

'It must have happened earlier today,' Carly said, gently folding the grass back across the body to hide it from sight. 'Maybe at the same time that Rameses was attacked.' She looked up into the tree, wondering what had tempted the unsuspecting squirrel down to the ground. 'Hoody, can you see what I see?' she gasped.

There in the tree, squatting on the lowest branch, was a second squirrel. Even from a distance they knew that here was another victim of the vicious attacker. Still alive, the squirrel sat hunched, its tail curved over its back, its face mauled and trickling with blood.

Without stopping to think, Carly sprang into action. She judged the tree, spotted knots and branches that would act as footholds and began to climb.

'Make sure you don't scare it off!' Hoody whispered, hanging on to Vinny to keep him quiet.

'It's too weak to move!' Carly shunted herself up the smooth trunk, grasping at branches and hauling herself up. The branch where the squirrel sat was about five metres up from the ground. Closer to, she could see that its eyes were dull, its movements slow.

Soon she drew level. Now all she had to do was creep along the branch. The squirrel fixed its gaze on her, but didn't shift.

'Careful!' Hoody hissed as she made her first move along the branch. It bent under her weight, but didn't break.

She edged forward. Then she stretched out her hand along the branch. Her fingertips made contact with the squirrel's soft fur, her fingers curled around its body and gently she lifted it from the branch.

'OK, now you've got to get back down one-handed!' Hoody said he would guide her. 'Back a bit more! Can you feel the main trunk? There's a foothold just to your right. That's it!' Between them, they would get the squirrel down.

At last her feet touched firm ground. Carly took a deep breath and gave the wounded animal to Hoody. 'Let's get it back to the surgery!'

Hoody was running through the trees, back up the hill almost before she'd spoken. Every second was vital. 'Will your dad save its life?' he asked.

There was the alleyway leading up to Beech Hill, there was the entrance to the Rescue Centre. Carly held the door open for Hoody, told Vinny to wait on the step. 'He'll do his best!' she promised, calling for help as they stepped inside.

Then the emergency routine took over. Paul Grey came and whisked the patient into theatre. 'Superficial wounds this time,' he told Carly, as she stood to one side, anxiously waiting. 'She's luckier than any of the other victims so far. Lost plenty of blood, but her pulse is OK.'

Mel nodded encouragingly. 'Well done,' she told Hoody, who hovered by the door.

'Vinny was the one who found her,' he reported.

'Well done, Vinny. He saved her life!'

As soon as they were sure the treatment would work, both Carly and Hoody wanted to be on their way. But Paul Grey's comments on the squirrel's wounds held them back. He'd given her a blood transfusion and treated her for shock before he took a closer look at the wounds. 'She'll need a couple of stitches, but nothing much.' He shook his head and pointed to the type of injury. 'They're trying to tell me a dog did this!'

Carly moved in again.

'I mean, look at the shape of that.' He pointed to a long tear on the squirrel's neck. 'It's probably been made by another animal, but these teeth marks are too sharp and pointed for a big dog.' He peeled off his gloves and asked Mel to put the patient in a unit where they could keep a close eye on her.

Carly followed him into reception. 'And when you think about it, all the victims have been fairly small too.' She listed them on her fingers: 'Russ is tiny, even for a Jack Russell. Then there was Rameses, and now the squirrels.'

Bupinda listened in. 'But what about Mr Price?' she reminded them. 'He says he saw this German shepherd with his own eyes!' It was hard evidence to ignore.

'With his own eyes!' The phrase stuck in Carly's mind. There was something wrong with it, but she couldn't put her finger on it.

Then Steve came in after his long, tiring day. Hoody saw him first. 'Did you get the report on the cat?' he asked, straight to the point as ever.

The inspector nodded. 'Just made it in time. The lab was about to close.' He dug in his pocket and pulled out a form, laid it flat on Bupinda's desk. 'Let's see ... tests on blood groups, saliva, size, shape and angle of wounds ... He read on until he reached the conclusion. 'Probably made by canine teeth, medium-sized carnivore ... but NOT the work of a German shepherd!'

'Brilliant!' Carly grasped on to every word. This was good, this was firm proof!

'But Mr Price ... !' Bupinda reminded them again.

'With his own eyes!' Carly bit her lip. What was wrong with it? Suddenly she realised.

'He *can't* have seen a German shepherd attacking Rameses!' she burst out.

'Why not?' Paul Grey asked. 'Come on, Carly, spit it out!

'Because he wasn't near enough. He admits that. How could he know what sort of dog it was? He's too short-sighted to see it!'

7

Everyone at Beech Hill Rescue Centre was agreed: the stray German shepherd could not be the killer.

Even Mel reluctantly let go of the wild rumours that people had accepted as fact. 'I got a bit carried away,' she admitted. 'It all started with that newspaper article, and I didn't stop to think.'

'You're not the only one.' Paul Grey knew that it was time to act. He took Carly to one side. 'OK, now you can tell me all about it,' he said quietly. 'With this evidence from the VIU, and your point about Mr Price's eyesight, I might well be able to persuade the police to – shall we say – change their line of inquiry!'

She was aching to let her dad in on the secret, but first she wanted to ask Hoody if he agreed. So she went into a huddle with him in a quiet corner. 'You can trust my dad!' she insisted. 'He would never, never put any animal to sleep if he didn't think it was necessary!'

Hoody wasn't so sure. 'What if it's not up to him? What if the nutty woman with the cats says the opposite?'

'Mrs Simms? She's not nutty. She's just upset about her tomcat. But honestly, Hoody, once Dad shows the police the post-mortem report, even she'll have to agree to leave our dog alone!' Carly fidgeted from one foot to the other, aware of the minutes ticking by. Soon it would be dusk.

'Will he give it those antibiotics?'

She nodded. 'He could bring them when we take him and show him the dog's den. The sooner the better.'

Hoody thought hard. Finally he agreed. 'I hope you're right,' he said through gritted teeth.

*

'Steve can drive us there.' Paul Grey grabbed his emergency bag and made for the carpark. He'd got moving as soon as Carly had let him into the secret. 'It'll be quicker.'

So they piled into the van and drove down Beech Hill, across Beacon Street into the Morningside Estate. A couple of rollerbladers whizzed towards them, then swerved at the last minute as Steve jammed on his brakes. 'Where to now?' he asked Hoody.

'Under that underpass.' He jerked open the back doors, telling them they had to walk from here. 'Come on, what are we waiting for?'

They had to run to keep up, following Hoody and Vinny on to the wasteground beyond the underpass, stumbling over broken bricks, scrambling over the remains of factory walls.

'Watch that big hole!' Steve pointed out a partly hidden pit in the middle of an old concrete floor. Carly jumped it and ran on.

'You could break a leg if you fell down that.' Paul Grey kept his eyes peeled. 'What was that?'

A high whine reached them from beyond the next wall.

'It's our dog!' Carly gasped. Still alive. Still in pain.

'He's in here.' Hoody waited for them as they dropped one by one into the deserted yard. 'Don't scare him, OK?'

Steve nodded. 'You two show us. He knows you, so it's better if you go first.' He held back with Paul as Carly and Hoody approached the dumped oil barrels and pile of rubble.

Hoody went first, scrambling over the rubble. 'This is the closest I've ever come!' he warned Carly.

They were a couple of metres from the nearest upturned barrel, peering into the gloom. There was a smell of old diesel oil and damp, crumbling plaster amongst the bricks. Then they saw the dog watching them.

His head was up, his lips pulled back and his sharp teeth bared. The hairs on the back of his neck stood on end, as he peered out at them from the shelter of the nearest barrel.

'It's OK, it's only us!' Carly spoke softly and

ventured forward. The dog followed her with his eyes. 'You're not vicious, are you?' she crooned. 'You're sick and scared.'

Slowly he responded. As she drew near, with Hoody coming on close behind, he closed his mouth and waited.

'That's right, good boy. We've come to help.'

They heard the dog whimper, saw his tail wag feebly. He stared at them with his beautiful, sad eyes.

Hoody turned to call Steve and Paul, telling Vinny to stay where he was. The two men climbed the pile of rubble to join them. When they saw the weakened state of the animal, they lost no time.

There, in the dirty, gloomy yard, Paul Grey injected him with a shot of penicillin. He took a quick look at the injured paw. 'Looks like a splinter of broken glass, or something similar. It's worked its way through the soft pad on the base of his paw and made an open wound. That's what's got infected.'

Carly had one hand on the dog's neck. She patted him and told him to keep still. 'Can you get the splinter out?'

'Not here. There isn't enough light, and it's probably gone in too deep. We'll have to operate, maybe with a local anaesthetic.' He discussed with Steve how they might lift the dog out of his den and down the heap of rubble.

'We need a stretcher. I've got one in the van. Hoody, you want to come and help?'

Carly stayed with the patient and her dad as the other two went off, with Vinny trotting alongside. 'See, he's not the least bit vicious,' she murmured, stroking the dog's soft head.

Paul smiled grimly. 'So this is your evil monster that preys on innocent victims!' He squatted next to the dog, examining him closely. 'He's half-starved, for a start. And it looks as if he might have been knocked about a bit.' He pointed out an old sore on one leg, a small scar on his nose.

'It's not fair, is it, boy?' Carly pictured a life of cruelty and neglect before the dog's lousy owners had pushed him out for good. And now, to be wrongly accused of all the awful attacks in the park!

'Never mind. You and Hoody found him just

in time,' her dad reassured her. 'Once we get him back to Beech Hill, we'll be able to look after him properly. It won't be long before he's on the mend.'

But his comforting words were cut short. In the distance they could hear Vinny's bark. Then a shout. Carly looked at her dad in sudden alarm.

'Watch out!' Hoody came hurtling back through the underpass and across the wasteland. Vinny shot like a cannonball ahead of him. Then Steve's heavier footsteps followed. 'Get him out of here!' Hoody yelled. 'Quick, it's the police!'

Carly jumped to her feet. On every side the shadows seemed to have darkened and closed in. Which way should they run?

'Uh-oh!' her dad said. 'No way, Carly.'

'Quick, we gotta move him!' Hoody climbed the rubble, sending loose stones crumbling down. 'That woman's got the police on to us!'

'Bonnie Simms?' Paul peered down the tunnel to see who was following Steve.

Sure enough, there was a figure in uniform and Mrs Simms herself, marching towards them, looking deadly serious.

'We can't move him without a stretcher. He's

too weak.' Carly's dad had never run away in his life. Instead, he went to meet the policeman.

'She's mad!' Hoody complained. 'It turns out she was following us. She saw the van and made the police come after us. That's why he's here!'

They stayed by the dog and watched from a distance. Paul Grey and Steve tried to explain. Paul raised both hands, as if asking them to hear him out. But Bonnie Simms was shaking her head. She wouldn't listen. She turned to the policeman and almost poked her head into his face, getting across her point of view. The young policeman backed off a couple of steps, then gazed across at the dog's den.

'Oh no!' Carly cowered against the oil barrels as she saw the policeman set off towards them.

Hoody swore. He turned on Carly. 'I thought you said we could trust your dad!'

The policeman drew nearer, with Bonnie Simms urging him on from behind.

'It's not his fault.' All of a sudden, Carly felt a strange calm. It was like stepping into a dream, watching the blue uniform get nearer and nearer, hearing Mrs Simms's high voice. They stopped at the bottom of the pile of rubble. Meanwhile, Carly kept firm hold of the dog's neck.

'Listen to me.' The policeman spoke clearly and calmly. 'You have to get away from the dog, you hear?'

She stared down at him, felt Hoody hold his ground beside her on the top of the heap.

'I've got a muzzle here. I'm going to come up there and put it on him. I don't want you to interfere.' He swung a black harness in front of him and set foot on the rubble. 'If you two are sensible, I can get the muzzle on him without any bother.'

'You can't do that!' Carly spoke, but it was as if someone else's voice came out of her mouth. 'He's sick. You can't put a muzzle on him!'

The policeman's shadow had fallen across the barrel where the dog lay whimpering. 'Better to be safe than sorry.' He let the contraption made from nylon webbing dangle from his hand. 'Now just let go of the dog and stand back, please.'

'What are you gonna do? Have him put down?' Hoody's voice broke in, rough and angry.

In the dusk light, Carly could make out Mrs

Simms's pale face. It seemed to float beneath them, looking up at their every move.

'The dog's a killer!' she insisted. 'He ought not to be let loose ever again!'

'He's not!' Carly knew her protest was useless. 'You can't prove it. Please don't take him away!'

Her words faded. She felt the policeman take hold of her and ease her away from the dog's side. Then he stooped to fit the muzzle around his jaws.

The dog whimpered. He shook his head. But he was too weak to resist. For a second he looked up at Carly.

She turned away, her eyes full of tears.

Then the policeman gathered the helpless dog in his arms. He stood up and half-staggered down the heap of loose bricks.

'Do something, Dad!' Carly pleaded. She put her hands over her ears to block out the dog's loud whine.

'Not now,' he answered, shaking his head as the policeman passed close by. 'Let's wait until we get him back to Beech Hill. Then let's see what we can do.'

8

'They've caught the wild dog!'

'Did you hear? That killer in the park has been captured!'

Word spread fast. Bonnie Simms told her neighbours the good news, and took most of the credit for getting rid of the menace that had gripped the area all week.

'What'll happen to him now?' Mr Price asked Steve Winter after his final visit of the evening to see Russ. He'd watched the stray dog being carried in and put in isolation in a section of the kennels reserved for cruelty cases.

'The police want to make out an order to have him destroyed,' came the quiet answer.

Carly heard the reply from her position by the main door. She frowned and turned away.

'Good riddance!' The old man pulled his cap low over his forehead, preparing to set out into the chilly evening air. 'Now we can all breathe easy again.'

They watched him peer short-sightedly at the concrete ramp outside the door. Kind Bupinda offered him a hand to the gate, where the street-lamp had just come on. 'Mind how you go,' she said, watching him on his way.

Then Paul Grey came through from the kennels, having made sure that the captured dog was comfortable. 'Doesn't anyone have a home to go to?' He tapped his watch to remind Bupinda and Mel that it was way past home time.

But this evening no one wanted to be the first to leave.

'What happened to the policeman?' Mel asked. She too had seen him carry the muzzled dog through reception, recognised that the animal was far too weak to have carried out the recent attacks. Now she hovered uneasily by the door.

'He went to the station to fill in the form under the Dangerous Dogs Act.' Paul Grey sounded tired. 'Go on, off you go. There's no point hanging around. This isn't the first time we've had to put an animal down, you know.'

'When will you do it – later tonight?' Bupinda wanted to know.

The question sent a shudder down Carly's spine. She caught a glimpse of her own reflection in the plate-glass door, saw Hoody hunched against the gatepost with Vinny, staring in at them.

She couldn't bear to wait for the answer. Quickly she swung out through the door and crossed the carpark. 'Come on!' She met Hoody with the frown still creasing her forehead.

'Where to?' He followed, glad to get away from the Rescue Centre.

'To the park, of course.' Even if he'd given up along with the rest, she definitely hadn't.

'What's the point? The dog's had it.'

'Not yet.' This was grim, it was the worst day

she could remember for a long time, but it wasn't over. She told Hoody about the paperwork that the police had to fill in and sign before they could get Paul Grey to go ahead and put the dog to sleep.

Hoody caught her up as she turned down the snicket into the park. 'Why didn't you say? – OK, never mind. We'll do what we planned to do earlier, find the real killer!' Suddenly there was a glint in his eye. 'Then they'll *have* to believe us!'

'It's the right time of day,' Carly muttered. There was hardly any daylight left; just a tinge of dull pink behind the beech trees, and a rapidly darkening sky. She stopped for a moment, wondering where to begin. The park looked big and empty. In the distance, the still water of the lake gleamed silver.

A figure sitting on one of the swings jumped clear and came up the slope towards Hoody and Carly. Then a couple of kids on rollerblades skated through the main gates. They materialised out of nowhere. Three more emerged from the shadow of the football pavilion; another one from a garden that joined on to the park. Soon there were seven or eight gathered around Hoody. No one said anything. They just waited and listened.

'You want to help us find the real killer?' he asked in his gruff voice. ''Cos the one they've got locked up in the Rescue Centre is the wrong one!'

All faces turned his way. Carly recognised one or two from school, another girl from a house on Beech Hill. But there were some she'd never seen before. They all nodded and agreed to help.

'This thing is still on the loose!' Hoody whispered. 'And tracking it down could be dangerous.' He paused to let anyone who wanted to fade away while they had the chance. But no one moved a muscle. 'OK, we're gonna take different areas of the park, spread out and cover as much ground as we can.' He split them into twos and threes, told them what they should do if they spotted a clue.

'We'll all meet up by the council stores at the far side of the park in fifteen minutes,' he ordered. 'If you spot any sign of this animal, don't do a thing. Just come to the meeting place and tell Carly and me. We'll deal with it. You all know the stores?'

The kids nodded. 'What kind of thing are we looking for?' someone asked.

This time Hoody looked to Carly for an answer. She swallowed hard, then spoke. 'No one's sure. But the rumour about a German shepherd can't be right. It's something smaller. All we know is that it's got sharp teeth, like a dog. And whatever it is, it's got a killer instinct.'

'Look in all the bushes and the long grass,' Hoody advised. 'Keep as quiet as you can. If we make too much noise we're bound to scare it off. OK?'

They were ready. Carly glanced round in the seconds before they split up to begin the search. Here they were: a gang of city kids, more at home on the streets and in the shopping malls than they were doing what they were doing now, which was combing the park in the fading light, tracking down an invisible killer. It seemed impossible. For a moment hope failed her.

'Ready?' Hoody urged. He and Carly had arranged to stick together and take Vinny with them.

His voice pulled her round. 'Yep.' She forced

herself into action and started off down the slope in amongst the trees where they'd found the squirrels. Her legs swished through the long, dry grass. Overhead, a wood pigeon flew from its perch and clattered off across the park. In the distance a dog barked.

They moved stealthily through the park, searching in the bushes that bordered the lake, under benches and in litter bins. There was a strange quiet, except for water lapping at the edge of the lake. Once, the figure of an adult stood at the main gates and shouted a girl's name. The girl cut away from her partner in the hunt and ran off home.

'Ten minutes,' Hoody breathed. He'd sent Vinny off to sniff around in the walled rose-garden. In five more minutes they would have to meet the others empty-handed.

'I hope they've had more luck than we have.' Carly started to feel desperate. 'If only we knew what we were looking for!' There had been foot-prints in the mud by the water's edge, and for a few moments she thought they were on to something. But she'd taken a closer look and decided they were made by different kinds of dogs. 'Hoody, where did you say you found Russ?' She thought back to the time when all this had begun.

'By the stores. The place where we plan to meet up.' He whistled Vinny back. 'Are you thinking what I'm thinking?'

'We should try there!' She nodded and they set off at a run. 'Russ was attacked at about this time in the evening, wasn't he? So there's a chance that the killer is lurking round the stores again.'

'Let's get a move on!' He wanted to be there before the others in case the noise of them gathering scared it off. His long legs raced across the grass, ahead of Carly.

They soon came to the brick huts which were built round three sides of a square, with a gravel space in the middle for trucks to load and unload. The huts had wide double doors, except for one at the far side, which had a row of stable doors, each securely bolted.

'This is where I found the Jack Russell.' Hoody

pointed to the darkest corner. He sent Vinny to sniff around again.

Carly squinted into the gloom. It was hard to see where Vinny was, but she picked out his white chest, heard his feet patter over the loose gravel. Then, out of the corner of her eye, she saw another movement. She held Hoody by the arm and pointed to a low roof under a horse chestnut tree.

The animal on the roof was in deep shadow, but they could see the white tip of its tail and make out a pointed snout. It crouched low on the grey slates, its attention fixed on Vinny who was sniffing out scents in the corner of the yard. Slowly it crept forward to the edge of the slope.

Vinny hadn't seen it. He was directly under the shadowy shape, nosing at one of the locked stable doors. When he jumped up and rattled the bolt, to his surprise the top half of the door swung open.

The hinges creaked. Vinny went back down on all fours and veered off. Then everything happened in a flash.

The creature on the roof opened its jaws and

snarled. The dog reared up and saw it, too late to escape as it launched itself from the roof straight at him.

'Vin!' Hoody's nerve broke and he yelled out.

His dog was locked into a vicious fight. Both animals snarled and snatched, charged and rolled in the gravel together. They were about the same size and evenly matched.

There was no time to think. Carly saw a workman's spade leaning against the wall inside the hut with the half-open door. She ran and seized it, swung it above her head and advanced on the fighting animals. 'Unbolt the bottom half of that door!' she yelled at Hoody. 'I'm going to try and drive it inside!'

He did as she said. 'What is it?' All he could see was struggling bodies, sharp teeth, pointed ears.

'Hold the door!' She ignored the question, concentrated on trying to separate Vinny from his opponent. Whatever it was, Hoody's dog had come face to face with the famous killer. Quickly she brought the blade of the spade down between them as Vinny backed off to gain his breath. She could see a trickle of blood on his face before she turned to drive the other animal into a corner.

'Go on, Carly, you can do it!' Hoody encouraged her. The other kids had heard the fight and were running for the store. They gathered at the edge of the yard. He moved in and grabbed Vinny by the collar, as Carly drove the other creature back into the hut.

She was face to face with the killer. Its orange eyes glared at her. They were rimmed with black, its snout was long and narrow as it bared its teeth and snarled viciously.

Carly held its gaze, almost mesmerised by the amber glint of its eyes, the narrow pupils and the wicked black rims. But she wouldn't be beaten.

Angrily it backed away from the spade which Carly used as a shield, until she forced it into the dark, musty hut. Then she slammed the door.

'Great! Brilliant!' A cheer went up.

'How's Vinny?' she gasped. She dropped the spade with a clatter, felt herself go weak at the knees.

'He's OK. Are you sure you got it trapped?' He hung on to Vinny, his arms around the dog's neck.

' . . . What is it?'

' . . . Did you see its teeth?'

' . . . We heard the fight from right across the park!' The kids were breathless and afraid.

'Has anyone got a torch?' Carly wanted to be sure.

'I never saw anything like it!' A girl crept nervously forward to hand the light to her.

Carly switched on the soft yellow beam and swung it towards the shed. She could hear the creature snarling in fury at being trapped. Warily she shone the torch into the dark store.

The cornered attacker stood just over thirty centimetres high. Its long, thick fur was reddish brown, its tail broad and bushy. The yellow eyes blazed back from the spotlight, the white fangs glistened.

'Oh!' Carly whispered, fascinated by its bright gaze. She stared back. Here was their killer. Here was the creature of the night.

The torch in her hand wavered, the animal

cowered in the furthest corner. 'Fox!' she said faintly, before the beam flickered and died.

9

From the dark pavement they could see the fair-haired policeman and Bonnie Simms standing in reception at Beech Hill. The policeman held up a sheet of yellow paper.

'It's not our policy to destroy an animal unless it's absolutely necessary.' Paul Grey was still trying to talk sense into Bonnie Simms when Carly burst in with Hoody.

The rest of the search party stood at the door with Vinny.

'But it *is* necessary!' Mrs Simms insisted,

snatching the form from the policeman. 'Here's the destruction order. What more do you want?'

The young policeman shrugged. 'The way I look at it, it's better to be safe than sorry. I asked my sergeant back at the station, and he agrees.'

Paul took the form. 'It's not logical,' he insisted. 'You could see what state the dog was in when we found him. No way could he have been going around the park terrorising everything in sight!'

'So? He'd injured his paw. That could have happened just a few hours earlier. It doesn't prove that he's innocent!' Bonnie Simms was so convinced she was right that no other opinion registered.

'It was an old wound,' Steve Winter said quietly.

Mrs Simms glared at him. 'Anyway, it's all irrelevant now. We've got the form to have the dog put down!'

'Sorry.' The policeman washed his hands of it.

'Dad!' Carly stepped forward. Her chest heaved from running all the way across the park.

He stopped her by raising his hand. 'Too late,' he murmured.

'I don't see what all the fuss is about!' Bonnie Simms insisted. 'We've got the whole neighbourhood living in fear of another attack from this vicious killer, and all you can think about is trying to protect our main suspect. I should have thought it would be the other way round!'

'Meaning what exactly?' Paul Grey was weary. He hardly had the heart to argue.

'Meaning that, as vets in a rescue centre, you should be the first to want to protect people's pets. After all, as the police say, why take the risk?'

'Because we can't prove that the German shepherd is guilty.' Paul repeated the well-worn argument. But it was useless. He knew the scared pet owners would have their way.

'I can prove that he's *not*!' Carly spoke up. She wanted to grab the destruction order from her dad's hand, force Mrs Simms and the policeman to follow her back to the park.

'For goodness sake!' The woman's temper snapped, and she ignored Carly. 'Let's stop wasting time!' She wanted the dog put down as soon as possible. 'It's only a stray we're talking about. There's not the least point in letting him live. After all, even if he did recover from his injury, who in their right mind would want to offer him a home?'

Carly, Hoody and Paul Grey stood quietly in the kennels at the back of the Rescue Centre. The cages were full, as usual. There was a greyhound called Timmy, brought in while his owner was in hospital, and Mandy, another welfare case, next to a two-year-old Labrador and Border collie cross. Then a big litter of mongrel pups, all look-ing for good homes. The dogs pushed up against the wire mesh, crying to be stroked.

Paul had separated the German shepherd from the others, had put him in a kennel facing on to the exercise yard at the back of the building. That was where they went now.

'Switch on that light,' Paul told Carly, zipping his jacket against the cold.

As the light flooded his kennel, the dog strug-gled to his feet, one front paw heavily bandaged. The muzzle he'd worn hung from a nearby hook. He looked pleased to see them.

'Look, he's wagging his tail,' she whispered. 'He recognises us.'

Hoody squatted by the mesh door. 'I can't believe we have to do this.' The dog limped towards him, put his face against the wire and whimpered.

'If the law says we have to, we can't argue.' Carly's father sighed. 'He must have been a fine-looking dog once upon a time.'

Now he was thin and his coat was straggly. But his face was still handsome, with its large, pointed ears and deep almond-shaped eyes.

'How long has he got?' Hoody wanted to know. He reached his fingers through the mesh and softly stroked the dog's nose.

'We should get it over with as soon as possible. Tonight would be best.'

'No!' Carly refused to accept it.

'Yes, Carly. Leaving it until tomorrow would only make it worse.' He had the lethal injection ready, the small, windowless room was prepared.

She shook her head. 'What if we could convince Mrs Simms that he isn't the killer?'

'We've tried and tried, love.'

'*If* we could!' she cried. 'Would we still be able to save him?'

The dog's whines grew louder. It was as if he understood every word they said.

'In theory, yes. We could withdraw the destruction order.'

She turned to him. 'Then, Dad, wait until tomorrow, please!'

'Why? What are you going to do?'

'Something. I don't know what exactly. But just say you won't put him down until tomorrow!'

He narrowed his eyes, then reluctantly he nodded. 'OK. Tomorrow morning.'

He watched them say goodbye to the dog and promise they would do their best. Carly took the muzzle from the hook, then they ran to join the kids who were still hanging around by the front door. Shaking his head wearily, Paul Grey turned off the light and left the dog in darkness once more.

Bonnie Simms lived alone in the ground-floor flat of a big house at the top of Beech Hill. When Carly rang the bell, the light went on in the hallway. She came slowly to the door and began to unbolt security locks and chains.

'Are we sure this is it?' Hoody asked. He looked up at the flaking paint on the porch, the overgrown creeper that hung in loops across the front of the old house.

Carly nodded. 'I checked the number in Cleo's case notes.'

'Get ready for her to slam the door in our faces,' he warned. He'd argued all the way up the street that Carly's plan might not work.

'You got a better idea?' she muttered. Out on the street, the loyal remains of their search party stood and waited. The last bolt slid back, the Yale lock turned.

'Oh, it's you.' Mrs Simms opened the door a crack. 'What do you want?'

'We need to talk to you,' Carly pleaded.

'Nothing you could say would change my mind.' The door stayed in place. 'I've already lost one cat to the vicious beast,' she reminded them. 'When Cleo and her kittens come home, I want to be certain it's not going to happen again!'

'That's exactly it!' Carly was ready with her

argument; the only one that had a chance of working. 'None of us want this animal roaming around the park!' They were all on the same side, though it was hard to believe it as she stood, hands tightly clenched by her side to stop them from shaking. 'Don't close the door, Mrs Simms, please!'

Bonnie Simms must have caught sight of the small group at the gate. 'Go away, or I'll call the police!' she warned. The door clicked shut.

Desperate, Carly pushed the letterbox flap and spoke through the gap. 'What I'm saying is, it will happen again! Cleo will come home and the killer will still be out there, believe me!'

Silence.

'Mrs Simms, are you there?'

Silence again.

Carly let the flap swing closed. She hung her head.

'Hang on!' Hoody was still watching the door. He saw it open properly this time. Bonnie Simms stood in full view, dressed in a big grey jumper and trousers.

'What did you say?' She stared at Carly in disbelief.

'I said the animal who attacked Rameses will still be out there. We'll have put down the wrong one.'

'We can show you if you like.' Hoody jumped in to fill the stunned pause. 'Come with us. We've got all the proof you need!'

But he'd pushed too hard. Mrs Simms glanced suspiciously at the other kids. 'You must think I'm stupid!'

So he ran to the gate, collected Vinny and sent the others on their way. 'See!' He wanted to show her she wouldn't be in any danger if she came with them.

'Where is this proof you talked about?' She was still staring at Carly with a deep frown. The picture had changed: she needed to know if the neighbourhood really was still at risk.

'In the park.' Carly held up the muzzle and a torch which she'd brought from the surgery. 'Come and see.'

Between them they coaxed her out of the house, explaining as they went.

'We found a fox in the council store,' Hoody said. 'It looks like that's where he lives.'

'There are a lot of foxes in cities these days.' Carly shone the torch along the dark path under the beech trees. Inside, she felt jittery about what they would find back at the hut, but she wasn't going to let Mrs Simms know that. 'They raid dustbins, and they catch squirrels and rats. It looks like this one will attack *anything* that's smaller than himself.'

'He even had a go at Vinny,' Hoody explained. 'That's how Carly managed to corner him when he was too busy to run off.'

'Shh!' Carly warned. They'd passed the lake and were drawing near to the huts. Vinny's hackles had risen as he recognised the scene of his earlier fight.

'I'm not sure about this!' Bonnie Simms looked around at the wide, empty park, then at the poky, deserted huts. A thin crescent moon, partly hidden by clouds, cast hardly any light.

'It's OK, he's locked up in one of the huts.' Carly was determined to go on. 'He can't get out.'

'What are you going to do?'

'I'm going to put this muzzle on him and take him back to Beech Hill. But before I do that, I want to prove to you that this is the animal we're really after!'

Mrs Simms hung back as Carly trod carefully across the gravel yard, but curiosity overcame her. 'Are you sure you know what you're doing?' she hissed. 'Watch out, whatever you do!' She made sure she stayed behind Hoody and Vinny, but with a good view of what was going on.

'Can you hear anything?' Carly turned to wait.

Hoody shook his head. 'Maybe it escaped.'

'Don't say that!' It was more likely that the fox was lying low inside the hut. 'No, I think he's heard us and smelt us!' She crept on.

'What if it attacks?' Once more, Mrs Simms was on the point of running away. She listened closely. Then she shook herself crossly. 'What am I talking about. I don't believe there's anything in there at all!'

Just then the fox let out a cry. Halfway between a bark and a howl, it marked its presence.

Bonnie Simms jumped and clutched Hoody's

arm. Carly felt the howl stretch her own nerves to breaking point.

'Now do you believe us?' Hoody asked, wrenching himself free. He wanted to be in position to back Carly up as she opened the top half of the door and pointed the torch inside the hut.

'Ready?' She slid the bolt, heard the fox rustle amongst dead leaves and other rubbish inside the hut. 'I'll climb in with the muzzle. You shut this door after me.'

She didn't give the other two time to argue. This had to be done quickly, before the fox could leap for freedom.

The top half of the door swung open, Carly half-scrambled, half-vaulted over the bottom section, shining the torch inwards to dazzle and confuse the fox. Hoody slammed the door.

She was inside. The hut was about the size of a garden shed. It smelt damp. There were spades and forks against the wall, a pile of dead leaves in one corner. But where was the fox?

'Carly?' Hoody's muffled voice called from outside. 'You OK?'

'Yeah. I can't find him!' She scuffed at the leaves with her foot. Nothing. *Where else could he hide?*

She turned to see a wooden crate behind the door. The torch beam picked out scattered feathers, one or two small bones. 'This is definitely his den!' she called. There were even scraps of food scavenged from bins: part of a chicken carcass, mouldy bread.

There was another howling bark; so close that it rang in her ears. It came from high up. Carly swung the torch towards the roof.

There was a ledge stacked with old plant-pots. And there, crouching in the corner, glaring down at her and snarling, was the fox.

'Found him!' she called out.

'Be careful, Carly!' Hoody was at the door. 'Do you need any help?'

'No, thanks. Hold the door closed!' She would keep the torch trained on the fox, inch towards him with the muzzle held ready. When she was close enough, she would reach up and tip a stack of pots from the shelf, hoping that the fox would take fright and jump down. She would corner him from behind, slip the muzzle over his nose, and it would all be over.

The yellow beam caught the blazing orange of his eyes. His pupils narrowed to thin slits. Back went the lips and there were the white fangs glistening with saliva.

Carly stretched and tipped the plant-pots. They clattered to the ground. The fox reacted as if he'd been shot. She swung the beam around the hut and picked him out of the pitch-blackness.

He was down beside her, ears laid back, jaws snapping. Quickly, before he could spring at her, she got into position and dropped to her knees. In a flash she slipped the muzzle over the fox's nose and fastened it tight around his savage jaws.

10

Muzzled and trapped, the fox gave up the fight.

Carly carried him out into the yard, felt his rapid heartbeat as she clasped him to her. 'Take a look in there,' she said to Bonnie Simms.

'Ugh, it stinks!' She put her hand to her face and peered into the hut while Hoody shone the torch on the small bones that littered the floor. 'That's horrible!'

'It's only doing what's natural,' he muttered. He refused to be moved by the sight of the pigeon feathers and scraps of mouldy meat.

'Now do you believe us?' Carly's challenge made Mrs Simms back out of the hut.

'I'm so sorry!' Her face was pale and strained. 'I can't say how awful I feel about this!' She clasped her hands together. 'I was wrong all along, wasn't I? . . . Oh, that poor dog!'

'Yep.' Hoody stared at her. Let her think it was too late to save the German shepherd: it served her right.

But Carly relented. 'It's OK. Dad agreed to wait until tomorrow.'

'You mean, he's still alive?' Mrs Simms gave Carly and the fox a wide berth as she backed away from the hut. 'That's one good thing. But what do we have to do now?'

'To save him from being put down? You could ring the police and admit you were wrong.'

The frightened woman nodded. 'Anything! What else can I do?'

'Tell people the truth,' Hoody put in. 'Say what really happened.' He'd put Vinny on the lead, ready to rush back to the Rescue Centre with Carly and the fox.

So Bonnie Simms collected her wits and set off

towards her house. 'I'll do that,' she promised, almost falling over herself in her eagerness to get home.

'Come on.' Carly felt the fox's stiff muscles tremble. 'He's scared; he doesn't know what's happening to him. We'd better get Dad to take a look at him.'

'Then what?' Hoody let Vinny off the lead as they all set off for Beech Hill.

'What do you mean?' She ran with the captured killer past the lake, up the slope towards Beech Hill.

'There's not much of a future for him, is there?' He pictured another outcry after Mrs Simms had rung round her friends. ' "Killer Caught! Death Sentence for Savage Fox!" All that sort of stuff!'

Carly feared Hoody was right. She clasped the fox against her chest, ran the last few metres home. 'Let's ask Steve,' she gasped. 'Maybe he can think of something.'

'Foxwood Wildlife Sanctuary?' The minute Steve heard their story, he picked up the phone. While Paul examined the fox in a treatment room, he spoke to the very organisation that could help.

Carly held her breath. 'Did you see how scared he was when we brought him in?' she whispered.

Hoody nodded. 'You gotta feel sorry for the poor thing.'

'Hello?' Steve was on the emergency line. 'We have a fox here at Beech Hill. It's been causing havoc in the park at the back of us, attacking people's pets. The whole neighbourhood is up in arms. Can you take him off our hands?' There was a silence as he waited for the reply.

'. . . Yes, he's fit and healthy as far as we can tell. He just needs rehousing in a more suitable area!' Steve winked at Carly. 'You can? That's great. I'll bring him over first thing tomorrow morning!'

'Sorted!' Hoody gave a satisfied shrug, then took Vinny home for his supper.

'Foxwood is the ideal place,' Paul told Carly. It was early next morning, over the breakfast table in the flat above the surgery. He was slapping butter on to his toast, scanning the local paper for news. 'It's out of town in the open countryside; a place where the balance of nature can operate properly. The fox will be in his element, helping to keep the rabbit population in check.' He looked up from the newspaper and smiled. 'Well done for sorting out this whole mess, Carly. I'm proud of you.'

'And Hoody!' Carly had slept like a log. Not only was the fox's future secure, the death sentence had been officially lifted from over the dog's head. Mrs Simms had rung the police to withdraw the destruction order, and the police had telephoned the surgery to inform them. They'd all gone to bed happy.

'That's too much butter, Dad. It's bad for you!'

'I don't care!' Time for a mountain of marmalade. He heaped it on top of the melting butter.

'I'm off down to the kennels.' She could hardly wait to see the dog. Pushing her plate to one side, she headed downstairs.

She had him out of his kennel, hobbling on his sore foot in the exercise yard, when her dad followed her. He stood to one side, smiling, noting that the wound seemed to be healing.

'See, you'll soon be as good as new!' Carly let

the dog come up to her. She crouched down and stroked the long, thick fur on his neck. 'I wish you had a name,' she whispered.

'Why not give him one now?' her dad suggested. 'Since we're sure he does have a future ahead of him, thanks to you.'

She smiled up at him.

'What's it to be?' he asked with an answering grin.

Carly put her cheek against the dog's soft fur. 'Rusty,' she decided. 'To remind us of the rubble and rusty barrels in the factory yard!'

'Rusty it is,' he said.

'Now all we have to do is feed you up and find you a home, along with all the other waifs and strays at Beech Hill.' She sighed and stroked him softly.

'Take a look at this!' Paul Grey stepped forward with his newspaper opened out for Carly to read.

' "Killer fox captured!" ' she read out. ' "Exclusive report on the mystery Beast of Beech Hill!" '

'Bonnie Simms contacted them,' her dad explained. 'But look further down the page.'

' "Innocent!" ' She read a smaller headline.

' "Suspect Dog Reprieved!" ' Carly grinned. 'That's fantastic, Dad!' Mrs Simms had kept her word about letting everyone know.

'Read on,' he told her.

' "The dog, a long-haired German shepherd, is said to be slowly recovering from his ordeal at Beech Hill Rescue Centre. However, a police spokesman pointed out that the reprieved dog is a stray, found sheltering on wasteland behind the Morningside Estate. At present he's officially homeless, so anyone wishing to offer him a good home should ring the Rescue Centre for further information." '

Carly sat down, right there on the cold concrete floor. She looked up at the sky, beamed at Paul Grey, then hugged Rusty for all she was worth.

Inside the surgery, the phone had already started to ring.

If you would like to receive the Jenny Oldfield newsletter, please either send an A5 stamped addressed envelope to the following address, or ask at your local bookshop:

Jenny Oldfield Newsletter
Marketing Department
Hodder Children's Books
338 Euston Road
London NW1 3BH